A MURDER AT OXFORD

A 1920S HISTORICAL COZY MYSTERY

THE KITTY WORTHINGTON MYSTERIES

MAGDA ALEXANDER

HEARTS AFIRE PUBLISHING

CHAPTER 1

JANUARY 1924

WORTHINGTON HOUSE, MAYFAIR, LONDON

"Good morning," I said rushing into the dining room. At fifteen past eight, it was neither early enough to endure an inquisition from Mother, nor tardy enough for her to comment about my late arrival.

"Morning, dear," Mother answered, a greeting that was echoed by the other occupants in the room.

Father, as always, was deep into *The Financial Times*. As head of Worthington & Son, it was of vital importance he kept abreast of financial news.

Ladies Lily and Melissande, seated opposite from Mother, were chatting away about their upcoming debut which would occur in but two months' time. My sister Margaret, now the Duchess of Wynchcombe and Lady Lily's sister-in-law, would present both at court in front of their royal majesties. But given she was newly married and finishing her degree at Oxford, Mother had volunteered to take on chaperone duties for the two debutantes, a gesture appreciated by all concerned. This, of course, meant that both young ladies would remain with us for the course of the season. It wasn't a hardship for either of them, as they already resided with us.

Lady Lily had come to us during a moment of crisis. We'd offered not only sanctuary but moral support. As a result, she'd blossomed from an extremely shy person to one whose laughter regularly rang through our home. Lady Melissande had ended up at our doors when her chaperone had broken her hip. Her brother, Lord Hollingsworth, had asked us to shelter her until he could find a new one. As matters turned out, there was no need to find a replacement. Mother was more than happy to perform escort duties for her as well. She'd determined two debutantes to esquire about would be no more onerous than one. Not only would Mother hold at-homes for them, but would accompany them to every ball, breakfast al fresco, theatre attendance, and pig races, if any were held. I sincerely hoped no such event was scheduled this season as everyone ended up dirty and smelling like, well, pigs.

After I helped myself to breakfast consisting of shirred eggs, bacon, mushrooms, beans, and tomatoes, I took a seat next to Mother. "So, what's on the schedule for today?" I inquired of Lady Lily.

"We have fittings at Angelique's for our court presentation gowns." Her eyes glowed with excitement.

After years of being abandoned at Wynchcombe Castle by her horrible grandfather with only servants for company, she deserved every good thing. With her beauty and charm, never mind her illustrious lineage, she was bound to make a glorious debut into London society.

"Don't we, Melly?" She asked of the young lady sitting next to her. Since they'd both come to live with us, they'd become the stoutest of friends.

"We most certainly do, Lil," Lady Melissande responded with a soft smile.

Their upbringings had been similar. And yet, different. It had been Lady Melissande's mother's dying wish she be raised in a French convent. So she, as much as Lady Lily, had grown up away from society. But she hadn't suffered the loneliness Lady Lily had. The nuns had not only provided her with a classical education but encouraged her love of music which seemed to provide an emotional outlet for her. Consequently, she was everything a well-brought-up young lady should be.

"The two of you are going to take London by storm," I said, after biting into a rasher of bacon. Their distinctive coloring—Lady Lily's blonde, blue-eyed beauty, and Lady Melissande's auburn tresses and eyes the color of the ocean—would ensure their success.

"You think so, Kitty?" Lady Lily asked.

"Absolutely. London society won't know what hit them when the two of you make your debut."

"Will you be able to attend balls and such?" Lady Melissande asked.

"Absolutely," Mother said.

It was impolite to disagree with her, but I had to qualify her answer. "Some of them. Most certainly, the ball Margaret is holding in your honor. But other events will depend on my schedule. The Ladies of Distinction Detective Agency is quite busy these days." As co-partner in the agency, it was my duty to attend to that enterprise. After our last investigation had been resolved successfully, our business had exploded almost overnight. We barely kept up with the matters brought to us. I couldn't very well promise to attend every event of the season when my responsibilities at the agency might prevent me from doing so.

Father, ever the businessman, rested the newspaper on the table. "How is that venture proceeding, Kitty?"

I was stopped from answering by Lady Emma's breathless arrival. "My apologies for my tardiness. It was a rather late evening."

Lady Emma, my co-partner at the Ladies of Distinction, had resided in the top floor of our agency's building. But when matters grew dangerous during a previous investigation, Mother and I had convinced her to come live with us. Though there was no longer any peril, she'd remained, something for which we were all thankful.

"Case in point, Father," I said. "Lady Emma was doing a spot of investigation for a client."

"Ummm." Mother said, "Young ladies should not involve themselves in matters that need to be handled at night."

"It couldn't be helped, Mrs. Worthington," Lady Emma replied approaching the sideboard. "It was the only time we could observe this particular gentleman."

"Where did you go?" Father asked.

"Salvattore's. A gambling establishment."

Mother bristled. "That's no place for a lady of good breeding."

"Oh, you'd be surprised, ma'am," Lady Emma said, "at how many ladies of good breeding were present."

"You did not go by yourself?" Father asked. He was more concerned with her safety than the propriety of the thing.

"No, sir." Lady Emma said, taking a seat next to me. "Lord Marlowe accompanied me. He likes to lend a hand when the occasion calls for it."

The occasion called for it more often than not in matters that Lady Emma managed, so much so we'd taken to assigning cases with that in mind to give him an opportunity to assist. Of course, Lady Emma did not protest such maneuvering for she was deeply in love with him, and he with her, even if both were too stubborn to admit it. So, any opportunity that caused them to be thrown together was eagerly welcomed by both.

"Take the Rolls, Kitty," Father suggested, cutting into a sausage. "It's much too cold for you ladies to venture out in your roadster."

He was right, and I was thankful for the offer. But it did beg the question, "Don't you need it to go to the office?" Worthington & Son was in the City of London. Neville, our chauffeur, drove Father there every day.

"I'm working on a new client's financial portfolio, and this afternoon I have a couple of transatlantic telephone calls. I can do all that from home. Ned can deal with anything that comes up at the office." He most certainly could. My brother Ned was an equal partner at the financial firm.

"What about your visit to Angelique's, Mother?" I asked.

"Our appointment is not until eleven. Plenty of time for Neville to drive you to your place of business and return."

"I thank you both then. We are more than happy to take you up on the offer." I did wonder if Father's decision to work from home had been a rather sudden one, or if it had been on his schedule. I supposed I would never find out. What I did know was that he and Mother were loving parents who deeply cared for their children and anyone else who lived under their roof.

A knock on the door preceded a footman's entrance.

"What is it, James?" Mister Carlton, our butler, inquired. He remained in the dining room during all our meals to ensure everything proceeded smoothly.

"The morning post has arrived, Sir, and there's a letter Mrs. Worthington might be eager to read."

"Oh?" Mother said taking the letter from the salver James carried.

One look at the envelope with its foreign stamps, and my stomach sank. It could be from only one person—my brother, the archaeologist.

"It's from Richard," Mother said in a censorious tone.

I glanced at Father whose dismayed expression must have mirrored mine. Richard had not only missed Margaret's wedding but hadn't bothered to send his regret. He'd left it to his assistant to apologize. That letter explained Richard was at a critical part of an excavation and would not be able to attend. Mother had been so upset she'd forbidden us from mentioning his name at Wynchcombe Castle before Margaret's wedding.

She handed the envelope back to James. "Thank you. Would you put it with the rest of the post on my desk? I'll read it after breakfast."

"Yes, ma'am."

"Are you sure, Mildred?" Father asked.

"It's bound to ruin my digestion, Edward. Might as well do it in the privacy of my parlor."

He covered her hand with his own. "As you wish, dear."

A woof from the door alerted us to yet another arrival—Sir Winston, father's beloved basset hound.

"Edward!" Mother cried out. "You know that dog is not welcome in the dining room."

"Not to worry, dear. I asked Peter to bring him after his morning walk. He'll keep me company in my study."

"Woof!" Sir Winston seemed to be as excited as Father. He must have spotted the sausages Father had slipped into a napkin. No doubt they would be given to him as a treat.

With Father drawing fire, now was the perfect time to make our getaway. I turned to Lady Emma. "Ready?"

"As I'll ever be." She took a last sip of her tea and together we exited the dining room before Mother took further aim at us.

CHAPTER 2

LADIES OF DISTINCTION DETECTIVE AGENCY

"Thank heaven for Neville," I exclaimed stepping into the Ladies of Distinction Detective Agency. "If it hadn't been for him, we would have frozen solid driving across London." Although I owned a roadster, it simply would not do to tool around town in the sporty motorcar. Not with the weather as frigid as it was. So Lady Emma, Betsy, my former maid but now agency receptionist, and I had piled into the Worthington family Rolls Royce and had Neville drive us to Hanover Square where our agency was located.

"'Tis a cold day, indeed, Miss," Betsy agreed.

January temperatures had turned downright frigid. The howling winds did not help. It was a day for staying inside if it could be helped. Unfortunately, it couldn't. Even in the dearth of winter, the agency was busier than it'd ever been. After the conclusion of a previous murder investigation, one that had involved a royal prince, we'd been thrust into the limelight by the London newspapers who'd spread the word about our success in identifying the murderer.

As a result, we had more work than we could handle, even with the help of Owen Clapham, a former Scotland Yard detective inspector and now an employee of the firm. With every passing day, it was becoming crystal clear we would need to hire another detective.

"Shall I put the kettle on?" Betsy asked.

"Please," Lady Emma replied. A friend from my debut season, Lady Emma possessed a sharp mind and sharper instincts. When I created the agency several months before, I'd asked her to become my partner. A decision I've never regretted.

After hanging my outer garments in the ground floor closet, I blew on my hands eager to get them warm. Even with the three of us tucked into the back seat of the automobile with motoring robes over us, it'd still been cold. Thankfully, the building had gas heat. We would warm up in no time.

While Betsy organized the tea, I headed for my office to review my caseload—an errant husband, a missing will, and a suspicion of theft. And those were the matters I was involved in. Lady Emma's enquiries were at least equal in number to mine. But before I reached my desk, the telephone rang. As Betsy was busy with the tea, Lady Emma answered it.

After a short conversation, she ended the call with a heavy sigh. "Another enquiry. That's the fifth this week."

"What does it involve?" I asked, hoping for an easily resolved matter.

"Another prospective beau."

"We need to hire another detective."

"I agree," Lady Emma said. "But who?"

"Let's discuss it in my office."

But before we could do so, the buzzer we'd recently had installed rang.

Betsy rushed to open the front door. "Welcome to the Ladies of Distinction Detective Agency."

A lady stepped in. Chestnut hair ruthlessly wrangled into a bun beneath a serious wool hat. Bright green eyes that glistened, from the cold most likely, behind a pair of spectacles that sat on a very commanding nose. Her navy-blue coat was not of the latest fashion, but it was quality, and meticulously kept.

I greeted her while Betsy took her outer garments. "Good morning. I'm Catherine Worthington, and this is Lady Emma Carlyle."

"How do you do? I'm Lady Aurelia Holmes." The mellifluous tone was totally out of character with her outer appearance of a no-nonsense individual. It was a voice a courtesan would employ.

"Would you like some tea, Lady Holmes?" Betsy asked extending one of the cups she'd prepared.

"Lady Aurelia. I'm not married. And yes, please." She took it from Betsy and drained it in one go.

"More?" Betsy asked.

"If you wouldn't mind. It was a rather bracing walk from the underground."

Heavens! She'd walked from the tube station several streets away. It was a wonder she wasn't frozen solid. "Let's step into my office where we can discuss your concern. It will be warmer there as well." When we were on the hunt for properties to house our agency, we'd insisted on one that had gas heat. As a result, our offices were warm and toasty and remained so as long as we kept our doors closed, which we always did.

Even though Lady Emma had more than enough work waiting for her, she followed along behind us. She was probably as curious as I was to discover what had brought Lady Aurelia to us.

After we'd taken our seats and Betsy had brought us our tea, our prospective client explained, "It's my employer, Lady Thomasina Walton. Her relatives are robbing her blind."

"I see." Not the first time such an accusation had been made. More often than not, we'd discovered sour grapes were involved. I hoped this would not prove to be the case in this matter for I would be sorely disappointed. But then she said the magic words.

"I have proof."

"Do you?"

"Yes." She reached into her handbag. As big a one as I had ever seen. It was more a carpetbag than anything else.

In the next fifteen minutes, she laid out before us a brilliant case: a list of people in and out of the house, times and dates included, with a list of the specific items that had gone missing after those individuals had visited. The evidence was practically flawless.

"You have been thorough," I said.

She straightened up and looked me straight in the eye. "I believe in doing my job, Miss Worthington."

"And what is your job?"

"I'm a companion to Lady Thomasina Walton. She took me in when no one else would."

"Oh?" Lady Emma prompted.

"May I explain?" She asked glancing at both Lady Emma and me.

"Of course," I answered.

"I was an only child. My mother died in childbirth when I was six years old, leaving my father, an earl, a widower. He possessed a brilliant mind and was more a scholar than anything else. Wealth was not important to him, so he handed the management of the family's fortune to his man of business. He passed away two years ago. Apoplexy, you see." Her eyes filled with tears. After taking a moment to collect herself, she continued, "It was then I discovered the man my father had trusted had mismanaged the funds. No sooner was my father buried than he fled to parts unknown leaving me with nothing but the clothes I owned."

"Oh, my," I said. "Were you able to appeal to the heir for help?"

"There was no heir, nor family, as my father had no brothers or sisters. My mother was an only child as well. With no one to inherit the earldom, the title went extant, and the small estate reverted to the crown."

"So what did you do?"

"Lady Walton was a good friend of my father's. Seeing my predicament, she offered me the companion position. I will be forever grateful she did. Otherwise, I would have been tossed to the street." She firmed up her chin. "That's why I can't abide what her relatives are doing to her."

"Have you made her aware of what's happening?"

"I've tried. But she's elderly and too trusting. She can't believe they would steal from her. As you can see, I have ample proof. Every time they visit, something goes missing. Small things of value—silver, jewelry—items they can easily carry away. She has an extensive porcelain collection from the time she and her husband lived in China. He was a diplomat. They haven't realized the worth of those pieces, but sooner or later they will. And then I imagine those will be gone as well."

"Have you notified the police?" Lady Emma asked.

"I fear they wouldn't listen to me. One of her relatives is friends with the commissioner. And they will retaliate if they discover I've alerted the authorities. I was hoping by coming to you something could be done. I know you have . . .

connections with Scotland Yard." She addressed that last statement to me.

I stiffened. It was common knowledge I was engaged to Chief Detective Inspector Robert Crawford as the press blasted that fact every time our names came up. They alternated between putting the information in a positive light and dragging our names through the proverbial mud. Anything to sell papers.

"Please forgive me. I did not mean to insult you," Lady Aurelia rushed to say. "I was just hoping you would be able to gain me an audience with someone who'd be willing to investigate."

"We'd have to do that ourselves before we alerted Scotland Yard," Lady Emma gently said.

"Yes, of course."

"Now as for the matter of the fee."

Spots of red bloomed on Lady Aurelia's cheeks. "I'm afraid I don't have much, only my salary."

"Oh, not to worry," I assured her. "It's the challenge of the thing that interests us. Don't you agree, Lady Emma?"

"Absolutely." Thank heaven she got the hint. "When would be a good time to visit?"

"Today, if possible. I've put it about that Lady Walton is ill with the influenza. They're all deadly afraid of catching something. So, they'll stay away until I say she's recuperated. Could you spare the time?"

Not really. Not only did I have other matters to attend to, but I had no wish to venture out in this weather. But needs must. "Of course."

"Wonderful." Her face lit up with a smile. "You should bundle up. It's beyond frigid out there."

"I will," I said coming to my feet. "But we will be hailing a taxicab." It might not be a Rolls, but it was worlds better than a walk to the underground.

Two hours later, I returned to the agency thoroughly convinced of the perfidy of Lady Walton's relatives.

"How did it go?" Lady Emma asked emerging from her office.

"She was right," I said after peeling off my leather gloves and handing my coat and cloche hat to Betsy. "They are stealing from Lady Walton. Such a sweet person. Still possesses all her faculties, but physically she has a difficult time getting around. She's in a wheelchair. Hardly leaves her room. So, she's not aware of what happens below stairs. Lady Aurelia tried once more to explain the thefts, but she refuses to believe the worst of her relatives."

"What can we do?"

"I'll call Robert and explain the situation. He'll make sure someone investigates."

CHAPTER 3

LADY AURELIA HOLMES

I wasted no time telephoning Robert about the thefts of Lady Walton's belongings. After he promised he'd send someone to investigate, I notified Lady Aurelia. Having done as much as we could in this matter, we got on with the pressing matters the agency had been hired to investigate.

A fortnight later, she reached out to us with some rather sad news. Lady Walton had passed away in her sleep. With her death, the investigation would not proceed as there would be no complainant.

After offering my condolences, I asked her to keep me apprised as to her situation. I was worried she would be dismissed. Indeed, that proved to be the case as I discovered a week later. The rapacious relative who'd inherited Lady Walton's townhouse had informed Lady Aurelia her services were no longer required and gave her a week to clear out.

She planned to move to temporary rooms until she found other employment.

Without consulting Lady Emma, I made a spur-of-the-moment decision. "I may have a position for you. Could you come to our office tomorrow, say ten o'clock?"

"Yes, of course." The poor thing sounded despondent. But I hoped my offer would brighten her day.

As soon as I ended the conversation, I sought out Lady Emma. Her door was closed, and a placard hung from the doorknob, a sign she was with a client. So, I had to possess myself of patience. I did not have long to wait. Ten minutes later, a lady stormed out of her office and flounced out the agency's door.

I found Lady Emma face down on her desk. She wasn't dead, only despondent. "Was that Lady Sheffingham?"

She straightened up. "Yes."

Betsy who'd followed behind me asked, "Would you like a cuppa, Miss? You look done in."

"Yes, please."

"Back in a tick," Betsy said.

"What happened?" I asked taking a seat on the chair across from her desk.

"I told her the truth."

Two weeks before, Lady Sheffingham, suspecting her husband of infidelity, had asked us to investigate. We'd assigned the case to Mister Clapham as he was the one who usually handled those types of cases. No evidence of infidelity had been found. On the other hand, there was plenty of it on her side. Lady Sheffingham was conducting an affair, with her footman of all people. "That we failed to discover any proof her husband was carrying on with another woman?"

"Yes. As you saw, she's not happy about it. She was

depending on us to find it so she could start divorce proceedings."

"So she could do what? Marry her footman?"

Lady Emma laughed. "I doubt she'd be that stupid. It would ruin her social standing."

"So would getting a divorce."

"Only temporarily. Many members of the nobility are divorcing these days. So, it's become more socially accepted. She could simply take a sabbatical and return in a year. By then the scandal would have died down. Or so she figured." She glanced down at her hands. "She refuses to pay the rest of our fee."

"We'll just go to Lord Sheffingham with the information we discovered. I'm sure he'd love to find out what his wife is up to."

Lady Emma's mouth twisted. "You know very well we can't betray a client's confidence, Kitty."

"You know that, and I know that, but does she?"

"She does."

"Well, at least she did pay a generous retainer."

"Which won't be enough to cover our expenses."

"We could always sue," I suggested.

"No, that won't work. It would bring too much notoriety to the agency."

"Hmm, you do have a point." I sat up and steepled my hands on the desk. "Let's defer that for now. I had an idea I wanted to discuss with you."

"Oh?"

"Lady Aurelia Holmes."

Betsy stepped into the room carrying a tray laden with teacups and a plate piled high with biscuits. "Thought you could use some sustenance."

"You are an angel, Betsy," Lady Emma said.

"Ta, Miss." A quick curtsy, and she was out the door.

"What about Lady Aurelia?" Lady Emma asked after gobbling down a biscuit.

"I want to hire her. Now before you say no—"

She sipped her tea. "I was not about to say any such thing."

"You saw the exemplary work she did on behalf of her employer. She was meticulous about her record keeping and presented the information in a logical, methodical manner."

"She did."

"We are overextended. With the season only two months away, we are bound to get more work."

"I agree."

"I asked her to come in tomorrow at ten. Will you be available? I'd like both of us to talk to her."

"I'll make the time."

"Fabulous." We spent another half hour or so crafting the offer we would make to our potential recruit.

The following morning, our prospective employee arrived a few minutes before ten, dressed as before in her navy-blue coat and wool hat. Seemingly, she had a limited wardrobe. If she accepted our offer, her new salary would allow her to buy some new pieces.

After Betsy took her outer garments, we proceeded to the conference room on the first floor where Betsy had arranged tea and biscuits. We allowed sufficient time to partake of the refreshments and discuss that old chestnut of British society, the weather, before I led off the conversation.

"Thank you for agreeing to see us, Lady Aurelia."

She folded her hands on her lap. "I was happy to come. As there's little for me to do, my time is my own."

"Lady Emma and I have discussed your very admirable qualities." While I proceeded to enumerate them, she remained still, but there was a glow about her which told me she was secretly pleased.

"Thank you for noticing them. It's not often people do."

"Well, we have been very impressed by you. So much so, we'd love to offer you a position at our detective agency."

Her eyes lit up. "As what?"

"Assistant lady detective." Lady Emma and I had discussed the position and had decided to give it that title. Hopefully, the 'assistant' would not overwhelm her and encourage her to accept our offer.

Her brow wrinkled. "But I know nothing about the detective business."

"Neither did we when we first got started," Lady Emma rushed to say. "We learned as we went along. We also have the very excellent Mister Clapham, a former Scotland Yard detective inspector, to guide us."

"But you'd already involved yourselves in previous investigations. I only have the one, and I was acquainted with the individuals."

"We encountered that obstacle ourselves. But we managed to navigate it, quite successfully I might add. People are very often willing to talk once you present them with your credentials and purpose."

"But I don't possess any credentials."

"You do. Since your father was an earl, you're entitled to be addressed as Lady Aurelia. That goes a long way toward acceptance. For those who are not impressed by the title, we've discovered other ways of getting to the truth."

She pondered our words for a few moments before finally gazing straight at us. "Do you really think it would work?"

"Absolutely," I fashioned a smile to put her at ease. "Does our offer meet with your approval?"

"I'm tempted. Sorely tempted." She swallowed hard. "May I enquire as to the salary?"

"Of course." Employing our considerable talents, we'd

discovered what she'd earned. Lady Walton's pay had been acceptable for a lady companion but not generous. We quoted her three times that salary. It would provide her with enough funds to lead a comfortable existence and something extra to indulge herself now and then.

"Oh, my!" Lady Aurelia said, her cheeks blooming with pleasure.

"And that's not all. When you satisfactorily conclude a matter, we will add a bonus. The amount will depend on the case itself."

"Yes, of course."

"There is an additional enticement we wish to offer. As you can see, the townhouse has three levels. Lady Emma used to occupy the top floor as her private quarters. But she came to live with us at Worthington Manor as it better suited her needs. But that floor is available for your use if you wish. Rent free, of course. It would help us immensely if you would keep an eye on the place during nonbusiness hours. How does that sound?"

She seemed slightly taken aback. "Thank you. I'm overwhelmed by your generosity. But I do have a few questions if I may."

"Ask away," I said.

"Would I have my own office?"

"You will. Right on this level. Right now, it functions as a library, but we can cart away the books so you can convert it into your own space."

"Oh, please don't remove them. I love books. They've always been a source of comfort to me. My father loved them, you see."

I squeezed her hands which she'd had clenched on the conference table. "Well, then they'll remain."

"There is one more thing. May I see the top floor?"

"Of course," Lady Emma said. She led the way up the

stairs, chatting all the while about all the features to be found. "You'll enjoy your own private bedroom and bathroom with a claw-footed tub. Although it does not have any cooking facilities, you can use the hob in the fireplace, to make tea."

"Are there cooking facilities in the building?"

"A cast iron monstrosity in the basement. We don't use it. We wouldn't know how," Lady Emma said with a laugh. "You won't starve. We have arrangements with the restaurants in the area to deliver midday meals. We can certainly extend it to include supper as well. We do have quite a variety of places to eat—not only British pub fare, but Italian, Indian, and other cuisines. The Tea and Tattle shoppe will gladly deliver breakfast fare as well."

Lady Aurelia's hands flew to her face. "I don't know what to say."

"How about yes?"

She flung open her arms. "Yes. With all my heart."

"Fabulous. When would you like to start?"

"Tomorrow?" A worry line suddenly appeared between her eyes. "Or is that too soon?"

"Tomorrow would be perfect. I can send Neville our chauffeur to pick you up. Say ten o'clock?" I hoped Mother would have no need of him. If she did, I would just have to make different arrangements.

"Thank you, Lady Emma. Miss Worthington. I can't tell you how thrilled I am. For the first time in a long while, I feel hopeful about my future."

"You're most welcome." I had no doubt she would make a wonderful addition to our agency.

CHAPTER 4

A VALUABLE DETECTIVE INDEED

Indeed, that proved to be the case. Within a week after her arrival, Lady Aurelia demonstrated what an asset she was. Having heard about Lady Sheffingham's refusal to pay our fee, she insisted on paying her a visit. Two hours later, she returned triumphant with a bank draft which paid the account in full.

Lady Emma, who kept track of our income and expenses took one look at it and exclaimed. "Why, it's more than the amount due us!"

"I informed her since she hadn't paid her invoice on time, she'd incurred a five percent late fee."

"But how did you convince her to pay in the first place?"

While I remained standing, Lady Aurelia took a seat across from Lady Emma. "Well, two years ago, when Lady Walton was still able to engage in a social agenda, she'd received an invitation to one of Lady Sheffingham's teas. She was happy to accept as she enjoyed such events. As the day was a fine spring one, I asked if I could deliver her acceptance. Unfortunately, upon my arrival at Sheffingham House, I had an urgent call of nature."

"Oh, how calamitous," Lady Emma said.

"Yes, it was rather. As I was in an unfamiliar house, I had no inkling where the facilities were located. So I asked and received permission to visit the necessary. Well, I took a wrong turn and ended up in Lady Sheffingham's private quarters. Imagine my surprise when I opened the door and found her in a rather large bathtub with a man not her husband."

"No!" I exclaimed, clamping my hand over my mouth trying hard not to giggle.

"Absolutely. I'd met Lord Sheffingham. An older-grey-haired gentleman, very dignified. The male person in the tub had a strapping physique and a shock of red locks."

"The footman!" Lady Emma declared all wide-eyed.

"Well, that rather makes sense, doesn't it," I said. "What did you do?"

"I retreated as quickly as possible and found a maid who pointed me in the right direction. After taking care of my need, I stepped into the hallway to find Lady Sheffingham standing sentinel outside the door. She made it very clear I was not to speak a word of what I'd seen. If I did, she would go to Lady Walton and demand I be dismissed. Of course, I readily agreed and made my escape as swiftly as I could. I never revealed what I saw. But now, since I'm no longer employed by Lady Walton, I do not see the need to remain silent any longer. And so, I informed her."

"Well done, Lady Aurelia," I said.

"But that was years ago, why would she care now?" Lady Emma asked.

"Lord Sheffingham is in contention to be the First Lord of the Admiralty. If it were known that his wife engages in illicit affairs, he would be passed over for another candidate."

"I fear we've made an enemy of her, though."

She sniffed. "Oh, not to worry, Lady Emma. I informed her if we heard one bad word about the agency which could be traced to her, my lips would be unsealed. Frankly, I feel that's bound to happen no matter what. Her tête-à-têtes with her footman are common knowledge among her staff. Sooner or later word is bound to leak out. When that happens, Lord Sheffingham will more than likely banish her to their country estate."

"If not outright divorce her," I said.

"Well, in that case, he'd be in the right. He could cut her off without a penny," Lady Aurelia said.

I laughed. "Remind me never to get on your bad side."

"Oh, you couldn't, Miss Worthington."

"Do please call me Kitty."

She flushed with pleasure. "Kitty then. I enjoyed myself immensely crossing swords with her. More than I've done in years. But it is more than that." She glanced around the space. "Strangely enough, I feel like I've come home."

I pressed her shoulder. "And so it is."

The next week proceeded more smoothly than any time since we'd opened our doors. At first, we took on the more challenging matters and assigned Lady Aurelia the more mundane ones. But she was so efficient in dealing with solicitors, bank managers, and household staff, we soon allowed her to take the lead on cases which involved such interactions. Two weeks later, we wondered how we'd ever done without her.

As we were constantly talking about Lady Aurelia at home, Mother insisted we invite her to supper. She very much wanted to meet our newest lady detective. Initially, Lady Aurelia demurred as she did not have an extensive wardrobe. But I informed her that was no barrier. As she was close to me in weight and height, it was only a matter of her choosing one of my gowns to wear.

"But I couldn't take your clothes!" She declared.

"I assure you I not only have an entire wardrobe of new frocks, but an attic full of them. I'm just glad to see them put to good use."

"No sense in arguing with Kitty," Lady Emma said, "She did the same with me, except in my case it was her sister's gowns. Half my wardrobe is comprised of them."

"You don't mind?" Lady Aurelia asked me.

"No. You'd be doing me a favor, really." The next day I had Neville deliver a trunk full of last season's gowns. I'd asked a seamstress from Angelique's to tend to Lady Aurelia. She would fit at least four afternoon and day dresses to her measurements as well as two evening gowns.

On the night of the supper, we left work early so we could bathe and dress at home. Filled with excitement, Lady Emma and I gathered in my bedroom to await Lady Aurelia. Promptly at eight, she emerged from the room assigned to her a totally different person.

"How do I look?" she asked somewhat shyly.

"Oh, my goodness, Lady Aurelia, you look magnificent," I said. The blue azure frock she'd chosen to wear suited her coloring no end and made her chestnut hair shine that much brighter.

We'd asked our family and friends to gather in the drawing room before us. Although the three of us descended the stairs in unison, we asked her to hold back so Carlton could announce her. And then finally it was time for her to make her grand entrance.

"Lady Aurelia Holmes," he said in stentorian tones as he rose to the occasion.

Everyone watched as she stepped into the room. Mother,

Father, my brother Ned, Ladies Lily and Melissande, Lords Marlowe and Hollingsworth, and of course, Detective Inspector Robert Crawford, my fiancé.

Holding out her hands in greeting, Mother was the first to step forward. "My dear, it is such a pleasure to finally meet you. Welcome to our home."

"Lady Aurelia." Father bowed over her hand.

Lady Emma and I made the rounds as we introduced her. Everyone had something pleasant to say. All the ladies sang praises over her gown while the gentlemen properly bowed to her. Once the introductions had been conducted, someone handed her a cocktail. Dinner was soon announced, and we proceeded to the dining room where we all enjoyed a wonderful meal and drank some rather splendid wine.

That evening was the last I would enjoy for a long time.

Two days later, a telegram arrived at the agency from my sister Margaret. "You must come to Oxford immediately. An urgent matter has arisen that affects someone dear to you. Don't tell Mother. Don't telephone."

My face must have shown my dismay as Lady Emma asked, "What's wrong?"

I handed the telegram to her.

She glanced up with a befuddled expression. "Whatever could it be?"

"I have no idea. But it's Margaret. She's the most sensible of my siblings. If she deems a matter urgent, it must be."

"How will you explain it to Mrs. Worthington?"

"I'll tell her a case came up that requires my travel to Oxford. She'll demand I take a chaperone, of course."

"What about Mister Clapham?" Lady Emma asked.

"No. He's too busy with that theft case. I can't ask Robert. He's in the middle of investigating those bank robbers. So, it's either Lord Marlowe or Hollingsworth."

"Marlowe is at his country estate. His sheep came down with spotted fever or some such disease."

"Spotted fever on a sheep? How could you even tell?"

"Haven't the foggiest."

I tossed my head. "It'll have to be Hollingsworth, then."

He readily agreed to escort me and promised to call on me at nine the next day. The following morning, Hollingsworth and I boarded the train to Oxford. At least with the addition of Lady Aurelia, I hadn't left the agency in a lurch. But the ache in the pit of my stomach told me something was very wrong indeed.

CHAPTER 5

ECHOES FROM THE PAST

The train station was quite close to where Margaret and Sebastian lived, so it took no time to arrive at their home. Since Margaret was now married, she no longer resided on campus. She and Sebastian had leased a house in Norham Gardens, an area close to her college, Lady Margaret Hall. The house turned out to be a quite impressive residence, as it stood four stories high. To a casual observer, it would seem a bit extravagant for two people, but Sebastian had been adamant about providing Margaret with every possible comfort during her last term at Oxford. And there was no denying the house provided an opportunity for them to entertain. Something Margaret was keen to do, as she wished to cultivate the patronage of Oxford denizens for her women's causes.

A very distinguished-looking, silver-haired servant met us at the door. "Good morning, Miss Worthington. I'm Maxwell, their Graces' butler."

"How do you do, Maxwell? I'm Miss Worthington, and this is Lord Hollingsworth."

He bowed in acknowledgement. "Will Lord Hollingsworth be residing with us as well?"

"No," Hollingsworth answered. "I'm staying with a friend. If you could store my bag, the black with a red stripe, until I'm ready to leave."

"Of course, milord." He flicked a finger and a footman rushed off to retrieve our luggage from the taxi. Having issued that order, he turned back to us. "Her Grace is expecting you. May I show you the way to her study?"

"Yes, thank you."

"If you will follow me, Miss Worthington, Lord Hollingsworth."

We followed his very stately pace through the house until we arrived at the study where Margaret was waiting for us.

In front of her was a table on which an Underwood typewriter rested, as well as numerous books and papers. Clearly, she was at work on her studies.

"Miss Worthington and Lord Hollingsworth, Your Grace."

"Kitty." Margaret jumped up from her chair and heartily embraced me. The smile on her lips contrasted sharply with the worried look in her eyes.

"Lord Hollingsworth." She curtsied. He bowed.

Having gotten the niceties out of the way, she turned to Maxwell, "Can you tell Cook luncheon may now be served."

"Very well, Your Grace."

As soon as he left the room, I had to say, "He's quite proper. I believe he 'Your Grace-d' you several times."

"Very properly trained, Maxwell is," she said with a smile.

"Where did you find him?" She'd had a disaster for a butler at Wynchcombe Castle.

"Believe it or not, he came with the house. So did the rest

of the staff, for that matter. Well, except for my personal maid and Sebastian's valet. Please take a seat." She pointed to the burgundy leather sofa that took up a large part of the space. "How was the trip?"

"Uneventful." She probably intended to share the news over the luncheon. But I had waited long enough. "What was so urgent, Margaret?"

She clenched her hands over her middle. "The remains of a lady were found near Magdalen Bridge which is located on the grounds of Magdalen College."

A faint remembrance of something Robert had said whispered softly to me. That was the college he'd attended while at Oxford.

Wanting to find a reason that was not connected to him, I asked, "And you want me to investigate?"

Not meeting my gaze, she fiddled with her wedding ring. "You may very well end up doing so. However, that was not the reason I urged you to come." She lifted her gaze and looked me straight in the eye. "The lady's name was Ellen Clarkson, and she was once engaged to Robert."

The sinking feeling in my stomach hit rock bottom with a thud. "Oh." I'd known he'd been engaged, and that the lady's name was Ellen. Not because he had told me but because of a conversation Mother had overhead.

"The inquest is to be held tomorrow. I thought you'd want to attend."

"Yes, of course." Whatever was revealed was bound to affect Robert.

Several months earlier when I'd learned about Robert's engagement, I'd asked Hollingsworth about the lady in question as he'd attended Oxford at the same time Robert had. He'd refused to divulge any information. I doubted he would answer any questions now. Still, I had to ask. "You were acquainted with her, were you not?"

"Yes, indeed. She was a beautiful young woman."

"And . . ."

"I think you should talk to Robert," he said, not unkindly.

"Well, there's no time like the present." I asked Margaret to show me to the telephone. Once she'd done so, I put a trunk call to Robert at Scotland Yard, the most likely place he would be at this time of day. Except he wasn't. Neither was he at his Eaton Square address. I left word with his butler to have him call me at Margaret's phone number as soon as he arrived home.

By the time my calls ended, luncheon had been served, so Maxwell showed me to the dining room. "Robert wasn't at Scotland Yard or his home. I left word for him to call me here."

"Yes, of course."

The meal consisted of several favorites of mine, but I could hardly get a morsel past my lips. Once that ordeal was finished, we moved to the drawing room to enjoy coffee and tea. Hollingsworth remained only a polite few minutes. His friend resided on the outskirts of Oxford, and it would take some time to get there. After the meal ended, he'd asked Maxwell to telephone for a taxi, and it was waiting outside for him. He excused himself vowing to return the following morning to escort me to the inquest which was to be held at ten.

Once he'd gone, I telephoned Lady Emma. Without providing any details, I informed her the matter was urgent indeed, and I would be detained at least one more day, if not longer. She reassured me everything was well in hand at the agency, and I need not worry. Whether that was true or not, I did feel less guilty about leaving her in the lurch. My second telephone call was to Mother. After basically repeating myself, she reminded me to be careful. I assured her Lord

Hollingsworth would escort me the entire time, so she need not worry.

After I ended the conversation, I sought out Margaret. "I should have told them both the reason I'm here. But . . ."

She pressed my hands. "You couldn't find the words."

"I wouldn't know what to tell them as there are so few facts."

"You'll certainly know more tomorrow after the inquest. You can telephone them then. Hopefully before they hear about it from the press."

I didn't hold out much hope that would be the case. These days, newspapers seemed to print the news mere hours after something occurred. Hoping to beat the competition to a story, they would telegraph a headline to their London news desk to be included in their afternoon edition. Once the reporters returned to the city, the details were expounded upon in the late evening issue. Well, it was what it was. I could only wait to see what tomorrow would bring.

The following morning found Hollingsworth and me at the Oxford Coroner's Court where the inquest would be held. I'd been present at enough of them to know what to expect. The coroner would call witnesses including police, the medical examiner, and whoever had discovered the remains. Others would be summoned to provide testimony, especially anyone familiar with the whereabouts and movements of the decedent prior to her death. Who that would be I had no idea. I hated going into the inquest blind. Other than what the *Oxford Times* had printed, which was what Margaret had told me, I had little knowledge of the young woman.

Hollingsworth and I took our places in the gallery which was situated above the courtroom. The bird's-eye view would provide an excellent vantage point into the proceedings. After a fifteen-minute wait, several individuals were led into the courtroom by an official-looking gentleman and shown to a bench in the front which had been reserved for them.

My breath hitched when I realized one of them was Robert. He neither glanced up toward the gallery nor around the courtroom but simply took a seat. I wanted to run to him and provide some encouragement. Of course, that was not possible in this setting where every action was so prescribed. I bit my lip and swallowed hard.

Hollingsworth must have noticed my distress because he squeezed my hand and whispered, "Courage."

All I could do was nod.

The officer at the front of the courtroom asked everyone to stand as the coroner made his way into the courtroom and took his place behind the desk. After arranging the items that laid there—his notebook, pen, and such—he called his first witness—the foreman whose crew discovered the remains. That testimony was fairly straightforward. Oxford College was renovating the Magdalen Bridge boathouse, and his company had been hired to excavate the grounds. They'd been working in the area for about half a day when one of his men discovered the remains. As soon as he realized what it was, he stopped all work and notified the authorities.

The medical examiner's testimony was much more extensive. The beginning mirrored what the foreman had said. He'd arrived at the site at forty minutes after three on February 8. The body was wrapped in a shroud of sorts which he carefully removed. After a brief examination, he'd determined it was a young woman. But he could tell little more than that as the body was very decomposed.

"Doctor Burnell, were you able to identify the remains?" The coroner asked.

"Yes. Her name was Ellen Clarkson. Although we found no handbag in the makeshift grave, she wore a medallion bearing her mother's name." That information had somehow found its way to the press. So, the woman's identity was no secret.

But seemingly, the coroner was not satisfied with that response. "She could have given that medallion to someone. Surely, you would have obtained a second identification."

"Yes, your honor, I did. When she was ten, she broke her arm. There was clear evidence of that. A former maid and a friend of the family verified she'd indeed suffered a fracture as a child."

"Very well." The coroner noted something in his book. "Were you able to determine when Miss Clarkson perished?"

Dr. Burnell drew out the suspense by removing and polishing his glasses before propping them back on his nose. "It is my considered opinion she died at least nine years ago, more likely eleven."

A murmur spread though the courtroom. That time frame coincided with Robert's presence at Oxford.

"Were you able to determine the cause of death?"

"She was struck on the head by a blunt object. It crushed her skull." The murmur turned into a roar.

The coroner banged down his gavel. "Silence!"

It wasn't until the room quieted down that he proceeded. "Did she die instantly?"

"Hard to tell, your honor. So much time has passed by. She may have lived a few minutes, maybe longer. But in my opinion, the result would have been the same. Sooner or later, she would have died."

"Could a woman have done it?"

"A strong, healthy one, yes. It doesn't take much force to strike a blow."

"Very well." The coroner made another notation. "Was there evidence of other violence committed against her?"

"No. There was a slight tinge of pink on the shroud, but it

wasn't blood. At least someone cared enough to cover her," the medical examiner ended softly.

Or to carry her body to the grave.

"Thank you, Doctor Burnell. You are dismissed. Please remain in the courtroom in case we need a clarification."

"Of course, your honor."

"Is Oliver Clarkson present?"

"Yes." A young man in the front of the room came to his feet.

"Come forward, please." The coroner waved him to the chair the previous witnesses had taken.

After he'd taken a seat, the coroner asked him to state his name, occupation, and relation to the victim.

"Oliver Clarkson, I'm a research fellow in the Astronomy Department at Oxford. Ellen was my sister."

"My condolences, sir."

"Thank you."

"Now, Mister Clarkson, we've called you to this inquest because you're Ellen Clarkson's closest living relative. We'll need you to testify about your sister's actions and frame of mind the last time she was in your presence."

"Yes, sir."

"When was the last time you saw your sister?"

"The summer of 1913. I was on holiday from boarding school. I was fourteen at the time."

"I understand something happened that summer."

"Yes, my—our father died from a fatal heart attack. She was very upset. We both were."

"What happened afterward?"

"The funeral, you mean?"

"Yes."

"Well, it was very well attended. Father was very highly regarded by the Oxford community. Our family was there, of course. Professor Burgess as well. And so was her fiancé,

Robert Crawford. A decent chap. Ellen was very much in love with him. At least, that's the way it looked to me."

"And after that?"

"Well, we couldn't remain in our home by ourselves. So Ellen went to live with our aunt and uncle."

"But not you?"

"No. I was sent to Professor Burgess's."

"Why was that?"

"Ellen couldn't stop crying. They felt I'd be better off in a less emotional setting. I was returning to school in two weeks, you see. I needed time to come to terms with Father's death."

"Did you see her after the funeral?"

"No. I asked but was told it wouldn't be a good idea. They thought the sight of me might upset her even more."

"How odd," I whispered.

Hollingsworth's response was a slight arch of his brow.

"Who relayed the news you would be staying with Professor Burgess?" The coroner asked Oliver Clarkson.

"I can't rightly remember." He brushed a trembling hand across his brow. "I was in such a daze."

"So, you never saw her again?"

"No, sir. I never did."

"Very well, you may step down."

CHAPTER 6

INQUEST

The coroner wasted no time calling his next witness. "Is Mister Burgess present?"

"Here, your honor." A distinguished-looking gentleman came to his feet. Going by his dark, grey-streaked hair, I would guess he was in his fifties. Not only was he well dressed, but he had an air of authority about him.

"Come forward, please."

After Mister Burgess had taken a seat, the coroner asked him to provide his full name and occupation.

"Alger Burgess. I'm the Warden of St. Simpson College at Oxford."

"It is my understanding that you were friends with Professor Clarkson, the victim's father."

"I was. As we were both Oxford professors at the time, we had occasion to consult each other. We became friends as a result. I was often a guest at his home."

"So you knew Ellen Clarkson?"

"Yes, indeed. She returned home once she finished school. She must have been, oh, sixteen at the time. She kept house for her father. It was something she relished. She was a very properly brought-up young lady." His voice took on a somber tone. "I was saddened when I heard her remains had been discovered."

"The medical examiner stated they were nine to eleven years old, that would be 1913 to 1915." The coroner said. "Could you take us back to the last year you had knowledge of her?"

"Well, 1912 was a time of great joy for her, indeed for the entire family. She'd become engaged to Robert Crawford, a student of her father. An exemplary scholar with a brilliant future ahead of him. Professor Clarkson very much approved of the match. Unfortunately, that joy did not last long."

"What happened?"

"He passed away the summer of 1913. As you can imagine, Ellen was devastated. I tried to do what I could do, but I was no substitute for the father she dearly loved."

"Oliver Clarkson testified she did not remain in her home. Do you know why?"

"Her mother had passed away a few years before. As she was barely twenty-one, she could not live by herself. So, her maternal aunt and uncle offered their home. After her father's death, she fell into a deep melancholy which was made worse when her engagement ended."

"How did that come about? Do you know?"

"No, your honor. I was not privy to the details."

"Oliver Clarkson testified that he came to live with you after the funeral."

"Indeed, he did."

"Why was that?"

"Ellen was so grief-stricken by her father's death, her aunt and uncle felt they had their hands full with her. Poor Oliver would have been given short shrift. As it was only two weeks before he was to return to school, they suggested I take him. Of course, I agreed. He had, and still has, quite a brilliant mind. I felt I could ease his grief through scholarly pursuits."

"And did he in fact do so?"

"Yes, he did. He visited the Radcliffe Observatory where he befriended several individuals. That's when he discovered what his life's work would be."

"Good to know some good came out of that tragedy. Very well. You may step down, sir."

The coroner next called William Staunton who turned out to be Ellen Clarkson's uncle.

"Mister Staunton, when did Ellen Clarkson come to live with you?"

"The summer of 1913. After her father's untimely passing, my beloved wife, Imelda, and I took her in."

"Could you speak as to her state of mind?"

"She suffered from melancholia. Only to be expected after her father's death. We tried our best to help her, but she rebuffed our efforts. There was no consoling her. Her fiancé, Robert Crawford, spent a fair amount of time with her after the funeral. Even took her punting on the Cherwell to try and jolly her up. It did not improve her mood. Just the opposite."

"What do you mean, sir?"

"When they returned from that outing, there was quite a row. Yes, quite a row indeed. Apparently, he'd told her he was returning to London as he had responsibilities there. She claimed he was abandoning her when she needed him the most. That he deemed other matters more important than her. The argument ended with her storming out of the drawing room. After he left Oxford, she spent most of her time in her bedchamber, emerging only for meals and condolence calls. My dear wife, Imelda, who's since gone to her glory, did her best to draw her out. But it was to no avail. She grew even more despondent after that day."

"Is that when her engagement ended?"

"No. That did not happen until October, shortly after Michaelmas term began. That's when Mister Crawford returned to Oxford. I arrived home one evening to discover she was no longer engaged to him."

"Do you know why?"

"Well, sir, as I wasn't present, I can't rightly testify as to what happened. But apparently Ellen claimed she'd trusted him to do right by her, and he'd betrayed her."

"Betrayed her how?"

"I don't know. My dear Imelda tried to discover what she meant, but Ellen refused to say."

"Ummm." The coroner made a note in his notebook. "Now, sir, how long did Miss Clarkson reside with you?"

"Not long. After the engagement ended, she decided to visit her paternal aunt by marriage, Mrs. Clarkson, who lived in Plymouth. She felt the sea air would do her good. As she was of age, we had to accede to her wishes. I accompanied her, of course, as a young woman could not travel alone. We boarded the train on November 14 and arrived in Plymouth the same day. She was welcomed most graciously by Mrs. Clarkson, I must say, very graciously indeed. The next day, I returned to Oxford. I never saw her again."

"What happened to her?"

"She wrote to tell us she'd met an Australian, a captain of a merchant ship. After a mere two weeks' acquaintance, he'd proposed marriage, and she'd accepted. As he was due to sail within the week, they'd held the wedding ceremony two days later. By the time I received the letter, she was on her way to Sidney."

"She'd already married?"

"That's what she said in the letter. Of course, we telephoned to verify that had occurred. Mrs. Clarkson herself told us that it was true. Ellen had indeed married a sea captain and sailed to Australia with him."

"Did she contact you when she reached that continent?"

"No, sir. She did not."

"And you never heard from her?"

"No, sir. We did not. My poor dear Imelda was devastated. We didn't have children of our own, you see. So, she'd come to look upon Ellen as our daughter."

"Very well, sir. Thank you."

Appearing quite distraught, Mister Staunton strode down from the chair and resumed his seat in the front row.

"Would Mister Edwin Clarkson come up, please?" The coroner said.

A forty-ish looking gentleman with mutton-chop whiskers stepped up to the witness stand.

"Would you tell us your name and occupation, sir?"

"Edwin Clarkson. I'm a vicar."

"And what is your relation to Ellen Clarkson?"

"She is, was, my cousin."

"Now we've heard that Ellen Clarkson came to live with your mother on November 14, 1913. Is that correct?"

"Yes, sir, she did. She wrote Mother and asked for permission to come stay with us. Mother readily agreed as she was very fond of Ellen, even if she didn't see her as often as she wished."

"We've heard from Mister Staunton that Ellen married an Australian sea captain and sailed away with him to Australia. Is that correct?"

"No, sir, it is not."

A murmur rippled through the crowd which the coroner had to gavel down once more. "Silence."

The crowd quieted down.

"Please explain."

"She indeed came to live with us as I said. But not because she wanted to breathe sea air." He took a deep breath, let it out. "She informed us she'd been seduced by a man she trusted and came to us so she could heal."

A huge uproar erupted. It took several minutes for the coroner to gavel everyone to silence.

"She informed you of this?"

"The day after her arrival, she confessed all to Mother and me. She'd found it difficult to continue to live in Oxford, so close to the fiend who'd stolen her innocence. As we lived in a rather remote part of Plymouth, she felt she could find peace, away from everything that reminded her of him."

"Did Miss Clarkson reveal the man's name?"

"No, sir. She did not. Mother asked but Ellen refused to name him."

"Were there any . . . consequences of the seduction?"

"Oh, God," I muttered. "Please don't let it be so."

"No. There wasn't. A blessing if you ask me. It would have been a scandal of prodigious proportions, and it would have ruined Ellen's life."

The coroner sighed heavily even as he made a note on the notebook. "What happened after that?"

"After a month, she declared a wish to return to Oxford."

"Why?"

"Well, sir. She wanted to confront the man who'd taken her innocence. She believed she was ruined and could never marry an honorable man. I assured her that was not so and even proposed marriage to her. But she declined my offer. She wouldn't take advantage of my good nature, you see. So, in the end, I obtained a train ticket for her. No mean feat, as it was nigh close to Christmas, and the trains were sold out."

"Did you accompany her?"

"I couldn't. Mother's health, which had been frail, turned for the worse. She passed two months later. I found a companion for Ellen. A servant who was on her way to Birmingham to spend the holiday with her family. On December 20, I escorted both to the Plymouth train station and saw them to their compartment. I never heard from her again." The man retrieved a handkerchief from his coat and wiped the tears streaming from his face. "She was an angel sent from heaven, sir. I pray that God will punish her murderer for his crime."

"What was the servant's name who escorted Ellen Clarkson?"

"Mary Perlmutter, she was a lady's maid to a friend of Mother's. I have no idea if Miss Perlmutter still resides in that household."

"Mister Staunton said he'd telephoned your home to inquire about Ellen Clarkson's wedding to an Australian sea captain. Your mother assured him that indeed it was so. Do you have any explanation for that, sir?"

"Indeed, I don't. Mother was bedridden by that time. She couldn't have taken that call."

"Very well, Reverend Clarkson. You may step down."

Wiping the tears from his face, Reverend Clarkson did just that.

"Mister Robert Crawford. Could you please come to the stand?"

Suspicious gazes landed on Robert with the fire of a thousand suns. Dear heaven. He'd been tried and convicted by those in the courtroom before he'd spoken one word.

Still, there was at least one person who looked upon him favorably. "Handsome bloke, innit?" A young woman close to me said.

"'andsome is as 'andsome does, I say," an older woman offered. "'e probably murdered that poor girl."

I started to say something, but Hollingsworth shook his head.

"Please state your name and occupation."

"Chief Detective Inspector Robert Crawford with the Metropolitan Police Service."

"A copper! Imagine that," the young woman muttered.

"Were you acquainted with Ellen Clarkson?"

"I was. I first met her the autumn of 1912 when Professor Clarkson, my tutor, invited me to supper at his home."

"Did you become engaged to her?"

"I did. We grew closer as I was often a dinner guest of her father's. She was not only beautiful, but kind, and very considerate of other people's feelings. I thought she would make an excellent wife."

"And yet the engagement ended a year later."

"It did. It was a mutual decision. We decided we would not suit after all."

"Why was that?"

"That is private, sir. And it has nothing to do with her death."

The coroner looked rather askance at Robert. "What happened the summer of 1913?"

"Professor Clarkson suffered a fatal heart attack. As soon as I heard, I traveled north to attend the funeral but could not remain long as I had other duties in London."

"What duties were those, sir?"

"Before attending Oxford, I'd been an officer with the Metropolitan Police. They were rather shorthanded that summer, so I volunteered to help where I could."

"After her father's death, Miss Clarkson seemed to require your help. Didn't you think that was more important?"

"She was in the care of a loving aunt and uncle who

clearly cherished her. I believed they would provide her with the comfort she needed."

Even to my prejudiced ears, that speech sounded more rehearsed than sincere. Those seated in the gallery seemed to agree as frowns showed on many faces.

"Mister Staunton testified that you took Miss Clarkson punting in the days after her father's death."

"I did. It was a favorite activity of hers. I'd hoped to lift her spirits."

"And that did not happen?"

"It worked at first. But when I told her I had to return to London the next day, she became quite agitated. She did not wish me to leave. As she had grown quite upset, I deemed it best to return to her uncle's house. We did not part on good terms."

The coroner consulted his notes. "According to her uncle, on the day the engagement was terminated, Ellen claimed she'd trusted you to do right by her, and you'd betrayed her. What do you say to that, sir?"

"I can't recall her words. It was not an amicable parting. That much I remember."

"Ummm. Reverend Clarkson testified that Ellen Clarkson was seduced. Do you know anything about that?"

"No, sir. I do not. I would never have taken such liberties with Ellen. If I may point out, your honor, that statement will need to be corroborated."

Fairly vibrating with rage, Reverend Clarkson rushed to his feet. "I'm a man of the cloth, sir. Every word I spoke was the truth."

"I understand, Reverend Clarkson," the coroner said, "but Detective Inspector Crawford is correct. It will need to be confirmed." He gestured to the parson. "If you could please regain your seat, sir."

"When was the last time you saw Ellen Clarkson?" The coroner asked Robert.

"The day our engagement ended."

Given the medical examiner's testimony, the verdict was a foregone conclusion, murder by person or persons unknown. But the testimonies clearly implicated Robert in the murder. The engagement had been broken, whether by mutual decision or his had yet to be determined. She'd claimed that he'd betrayed her. If the cousin could be believed, she'd returned to Oxford shortly before Christmas to confront the man who'd stolen her innocence. Robert would have been in Oxford at the time, so, a clear implication could be made that she'd confronted him, threatened to expose him, and he'd killed her to stop her from doing so.

Eager to talk to Robert at the end of the inquest, I started to rush toward him, but Hollingsworth held me back. Newspaper photographers were madly snapping his photograph. My presence would only make things worse.

CHAPTER 7

THE INQUEST AFTERMATH

Back at Margaret's home, we relinquished our outer garments to Maxwell who informed us she was waiting for us in her study. We found her as before, surrounded by books and papers while busily typing away on her Underwood typewriter.

As soon as we stepped into the room, she came to her feet. "Kitty, Lord Hollingsworth, how did it go?"

"Awful," I said, dropping into a burgundy settee. "Robert was there."

A myriad of emotions rolled across her face. Concern, curiosity, unease. "Was he?"

"Yes." I gave her an account of the testimonies ending with the most damning of all. "Everything points to him as the murderer. The way the engagement ended, his lack of emotion when he testified. I know what he was doing, Margaret. He was holding back. That's his training. The detective in him doesn't give anything away. But it made him seem as if he didn't care two figs for Ellen Clarkson." I swallowed hard. "I fear what will happen."

"Such as?"

My voice broke. "That he will be charged with her murder."

She sat next to me and put her arm around my shoulder. "Surely it won't come to that, dearest."

I pinned her with a hard stare. "Won't it? I've seen others charged for less."

She folded her hands on her lap and began fiddling with her wedding ring. "Did you get an opportunity to talk to him?"

"No. He was being mobbed by reporters and photographers were snapping his picture. Hollingsworth held me back. Rightfully so. If I had approached Robert, it would have caused even more of a sensation." I glanced at Hollingsworth. "You will arrange a meeting with him, won't you?"

"As soon as it can be managed. I imagine he's staying somewhere in Oxford."

"But how will you know where he is?" My logical sister asked.

"I asked Salverton to follow him out of the courtroom."

"Did you really?" I asked. "Why didn't you mention it?"

"You had enough on your mind. I didn't want to add to your worries." He glanced at his watch. "I better go. We agreed to meet at the Bodleian Library at three, and it's almost that time now."

"Please join us for supper, and bring Lord Salverton along," Margaret said.

Hollingsworth shook his head. "Thank you, but I'll have to decline. Salverton arranged an evening with old friends. But first, I'll find Robert and arrange a time for Kitty to meet with him."

I stood and walked toward him. "Please inform us as soon as you can."

"Of course." He pressed my clutched hands. "Take heart, Kitty. Things aren't as dark as they seem."

If only I could believe that.

Shortly before supper, a note arrived from Hollingsworth. He'd located Robert and arranged for the meeting to be held the next morning at ten at the Prince of Wales Hotel where Robert had reserved a room.

"Why not here?" Margaret asked.

"He doesn't want to bring the newshounds down on you." I gazed off into the distance. "They're probably camped in front of Robert's hotel."

"Ahhh. But won't they notice when you arrive?"

"Anticipating I'd need a disguise, I packed one." Heaving out a deep sigh, I said, "Now, I really must call Mother and give her the news."

"Better you than me," Margaret said in a commiserating tone.

Mother took it as well as could be expected, with not one word of censure about my lying to her. "What are you planning to do?" She knew me well enough to know that I would not stand by and allow matters to play out.

"Talk to him. Hollingsworth is arranging a meeting."

"Why can't you approach him directly?"

"The press more than likely followed him back to the hotel and are keeping watch."

She asked the same question as Margaret, and I provided the same answer. "They won't know who I am as I'll be disguised."

"If you need anything, Kitty, please let us know. Your father and I will do whatever it takes to help."

"Thank you, Mother. That means a lot. I'll let Robert know as well."

"Please do."

I ended the conversation in a slightly better frame of mind. Whatever the future brought, I was not alone. I had family and friends who would stand by Robert and me. I just hoped it would be enough.

CHAPTER 8

ROBERT'S TALE

The following morning, I took great pains with my wardrobe to ensure no one would know who I was. As Hollingsworth was well-known to the press for his seafaring adventures and lectures at the Geographical Society, he would be instantly recognized. So, once we arrived at the hotel, I entered by myself.

Sure enough, I was ignored as I walked through the lobby and climbed aboard the elevator. Once I reached my destination—room 316—I knocked, and Robert opened the door. For a moment, his brow wrinkled. "I'm sorry, ma'am, but now is not a good time. I'm expecting someone."

Ignoring his words, I stepped into the room.

"What the—"

"Close the door, Robert."

"Catherine?" He asked after he'd done so.

I lifted my widow's veil. "The one and only."

"How did . . . you appear to have gained two stone."

"One of the many disguises I employ on agency matters." I'd grinned when greeting him, but I turned downright serious when I noticed the dark circles under his eyes. "How are you bearing up?"

"I'm fine." He wasn't, but, of course, he would say he was.

But now was not the time to challenge him. I'd come for another purpose. To learn the truth about his relationship with Ellen Clarkson.

"Why are you here?" He asked.

"I was at the inquest."

He whirled away from me. "You shouldn't have come to Oxford, Catherine."

"Why not?"

He veered away from me. "I don't want you involved in this . . . ugliness."

As if I would abandon him to face this crucible alone. "I'm already involved."

He whirled back. "Then uninvolve yourself." Not a suggestion but a command.

One I would not obey. "You know me better than that, Robert. I've investigated murders where others dear to me were accused or suspected of the crime—my brother, Sebastian, Newcastle. Why wouldn't I investigate a matter that involved you?"

"Because I'm asking you not to." His voice shook with anger; his eyes blazed with heat.

His emotions were running ragged, understandably so. But I couldn't fight fire with fire. That would get us nowhere. Taking a seat on the silk-covered settee in the sitting room, I said, "Tell me about Ellen."

He waved a hand in the air, a clear dismissal. "You were at the inquest. You heard what I said."

Stubborn, beautiful man. "You were under oath and provided the merest explanation. I want to know more."

He brushed a hand across his brow. "Such as?"

"How did you meet her?"

"Professor Clarkson invited me to supper. She was his hostess." He tossed a frustrated gaze toward me. "I said that at the inquest."

I retrieved notebook and pen from my handbag.

He pointed to them. "Do you have to do that?"

"You know I do, Robert." Ignoring his peevishness, I opened the notebook to a blank page. "What was your opinion of her?"

"Beautiful, charming, educated." He hesitated a moment before he continued. "She was soft-spoken, never raised her voice during the entire meal, even to the servants. But she made sure everything proceeded smoothly. After supper, she retired to the drawing room and left her father and me to enjoy our port and cigars. When we rejoined her, I found her embroidering something. A cushion cover, I think."

I couldn't embroider initials on a handkerchief to save my life. "And that appealed to you?"

"Yes, it did. She was nigh perfect, everything a young man hopes for in the way of a wife."

That struck me harder than I thought it would. I knew they'd been engaged, but somehow, I'd convinced myself she was wrong for him. His words said otherwise. Regardless of my feelings, I had to carry on. "And the more you saw her—"

"The stronger that belief grew. Within months, I approached the professor and asked his permission to propose to her. He approved. The day she consented to be my wife was the happiest moment of my life."

It hurt that statement. But I couldn't allow my emotions to interfere. To help him, I would need to approach it like any other investigation and keep asking questions.

"Please take a seat, Robert. I'm getting a crick in my neck looking up at you."

"My apologies." He accommodated himself in the matching armchair situated across from me.

The physical space that lay between us might have been small, but the mental distance was great. As if that would stop me. "What happened the summer of 1913?"

"After Hilary term ended, I joined my family in London. My only thought was to enjoy that time, unencumbered by the intense Oxford pace. But I ran into a couple of my former police mates, and they told me how shorthanded they were. How they could really use some help. So I volunteered my time. I felt it would improve my chances of obtaining a detective position at Scotland Yard. Lord Rutledge encouraged me in that notion."

"Yes, I know." While working as a police officer, Robert had saved Lord Rutledge from a gang of thugs who'd assaulted him. Robert had suffered extensive injuries as a result. It had taken him six months to recuperate. During that time, Lord Rutledge had come to know Robert well. He'd deemed it a waste for Robert to squander his intellect on the police force and paid for Robert's studies at Oxford so he could qualify for a detective position. As his family's modest income would not cover such an expense, Robert was immensely grateful for the offer. With Lord Rutledge's sponsorship, he had indeed been hired as a detective inspector. But the rest had been up to Robert himself. It was his intelligence, drive, and persistence that had earned him the position of Chief Detective Inspector. "Go on."

"In July I received a telegram. Professor Clarkson had suffered a fatal heart attack. I packed as quickly as I could and returned to Oxford. Ellen was, of course, devastated."

"She and her father were close?"

"As much as a daughter and a father can be."

An odd answer to be sure but one not to be remarked upon now.

"You stayed for a few days?"

"A week as I recall. I sought to provide her with whatever comfort I could."

"How did you go about it?"

"She loved to go punting on the Cherwell, so I asked the restaurant at the hotel to prepare a picnic basket."

"Where were you staying?"

"Right here, at the Prince of Wales."

I made a mental note of it. "Sorry for the interruption. Please proceed."

"It was an unusually fine day, sunny with not a cloud in the sky. We meandered down the river to a favorite spot of hers at University Parks. For that period, she put away her sadness." He brushed a hand across his brow. "Unfortunately, that did not last long."

"Why?"

"I told her I had to go back to London the next day. Her smile vanished; her eyes blazed with anger. She demanded to know why. I explained how shorthanded the Metropolitan Police were. During the months leading up to that summer, suffragettes had posted letter bombs which blew up letter boxes, post offices, mail bags. Naturally, that caused a great deal of unrest. The police needed seasoned officers to keep the peace. She claimed I was placing more importance on that than her. I assured her that was not the case, but she didn't believe me. As she had grown quite agitated, I packed up the picnic basket and escorted her home. She maintained a cold silence the entire trip back to her uncle's house. When we arrived, she resumed her argument. I tried my best to calm her down, but she stormed out of the drawing room before I could do so. I left. What else could I do?"

"And you didn't see her again until you returned in October for Michaelmas term?"

"Yes."

"You didn't visit her between July and that time?"

"I wrote, but no, I did not return until then."

CHAPTER 9

ROBERT'S TALE (PART DEUX)

"So what happened when you arrived back at Oxford in the fall?"

"My first visit was to her, of course. She'd . . . changed."

"What do you mean?"

"She'd become harder."

I didn't have to wonder why. If, heaven forbid, Father passed away, I would be devastated. But at least I'd have Mother, as well as my brothers and sisters, to lean upon. Ellen Clarkson had an aunt and uncle, but somehow, they hadn't eased her grief. That was something we'd need to explore. "The death of her father had to affect her deeply."

"It was more than that. She'd . . . developed expectations about our future. Since I was studying jurisprudence, she thought I would become a barrister or a solicitor and, at some point, run for Parliament. I told her I had no interest in politics and would continue to do police work. She couldn't countenance being the wife of a policeman."

"What did you say to her?"

"I explained I was aiming higher than that. That I intended to become a detective inspector at Scotland Yard. But all she saw was that I would remain a lowly officer of the law. She couldn't tolerate that from a husband and returned the ring I'd given her. Knowing how she felt, I agreed it was for the best."

"So she terminated the engagement?"

"It was a mutual decision, Kitty. I agreed with her. We did not suit. Not anymore. Maybe not ever."

He could phrase it however he wished, but clearly it had been her decision.

"Would you have remained engaged to her if she hadn't ended it?"

"I'd given my word, Kitty. I couldn't very well go back on it."

"You would have endured a life of misery rather than commit that dishonor?"

"She would have made a fine wife, kept my house, borne my children. It wouldn't have been total misery."

It wouldn't have been a joyful marriage, not the way she felt about his chosen profession. Seemingly, she'd felt that way from the start. Had it been a miscommunication on their part, or had something happened to change her view? I jotted down a note. It was a question that needed to be explored. "What happened after the engagement ended?"

"I went on with my studies. There was nothing else to do."

"People didn't . . . talk?"

His lip curled up with derision. "Oh, there was plenty of that. The end of our engagement became well-known. Oxford is a small town, after all. When she left for Plymouth a couple of weeks later, it changed from rumors to blatant lies. People claimed I'd ended the engagement, and Ellen had been so devastated, she'd fled."

"You didn't explain what had happened?"

"No. It was no one's business but our own. I figured the rumors would die down. And they did. Eventually."

In the meantime, he'd been pilloried for something he didn't do. Now that Ellen's remains had been discovered those rumors were bound to resurface with a vengeance. And he'd be blamed for something a lot worse than a broken engagement. "What happened when she didn't return? Didn't you think that was odd?"

"No. Not really. She'd been so unhappy after her father died. I believed her memories were too painful for her to return to Oxford and had sought a happier life."

He sounded as if he hadn't cared when I knew the opposite was true. Ellen had not been the only one devastated. He'd been as well. More than likely, he'd imagined a beautiful life with a wife who loved him while he pursued his career at Scotland Yard. And then it'd all come crashing down when Ellen had ended the engagement.

"You graduated the following year, did you not?" I was familiar with this part of the story but wanted to give him a chance to speak to it.

His restlessness drove him to his feet, and he took to pacing the floor. "I did. By that time, the Great War had begun, and I enlisted. A year into it, I was injured and sent home to recuperate. Rather than report back to the army, Father and Lord Rutledge suggested I return to police work as officers were desperately needed. Lord Rutledge used his influence to obtain a detective position at Scotland Yard. The rest you know."

I did indeed. He'd worked hard as a detective and had recently been promoted to Chief Detective Inspector. He'd chosen an honorable career and been rewarded for it. "Didn't you ever wonder about Ellen?"

"Now and then, but not enough to go in search of her.

She was but a distant memory that had soured at the end. There was no sense in raking over those ashes."

"Her family never contacted you?"

"No. But then, why would they? Her brother, Oliver, was only fourteen and away at school during most of our engagement. I met him at Christmas when he came home for the holiday and spoke but a few words of condolence after his father's funeral. And as far as Ellen's aunt and uncle, I only had two conversations with them. Once after the funeral and another before I escorted Ellen to the picnic. So, I put it all in the past and got on with my life."

The next question was bound to be the hardest one. I took a deep breath and let it out. "Were you ever intimate with her?"

A shocked silence met me, followed by a hard, cold answer. "Of course not. I would have never taken such liberties with her." He was so angry, he turned away.

I was causing him a great deal of pain, but it couldn't be helped. He had to realize what he was up against. "Others think you did. Her uncle certainly does. Whoever oversees this case will ask that question of you. You'll need a better answer than the one you've just given me."

He whirled back. "How could I possibly prove a negative?"

"We'll have to figure out a way."

"We?" He marched toward me and bracketed his arms around me, caging me in. "You are not getting involved in this matter, Catherine."

I hitched up my chin. "Why not?"

"Because I don't wish you to. It's bound to be a dirty, filthy investigation. Whether Ellen went willingly to some man's bed or, heaven forbid, was forced, there's bound to be a scandal, and I don't want you anywhere near it." Grabbing me by the shoulders, he raised me to my feet and held me tight. "I don't want you to be touched by this." And then he kissed me, and I melted into him. As heaven help me, I always do.

Ending the kiss, he rested his head on mine. "Please don't do this, Catherine. I'm begging you," he whispered. "Please."

His heart was beating so hard, I felt it thrumming against me. I had a choice to make. Deny him and risk everything we meant to each other or agree to his request. I couldn't lose him, so I gave him the only answer I could, "All right."

"Thank you, my darling. Everything will work itself out, you'll see."

He was wrong, of course. Whether he accepted it or not, he was implicated in the murder. Sooner or later, a detective inspector would knock on his door and bring him in for questioning. I would just have to wait and see it play out.

CHAPTER 10

AN INTERCESSION

While Robert and I returned to London on the next morning's train, Hollingsworth remained behind, allegedly to reacquaint himself with some old friends. I believed he was doing more than that. More than likely, he wanted to see which way the wind was blowing.

For the next few days, everything was fine, both at home and at the agency, although everyone was walking on eggshells around me, afraid I would break. Mother, Ladies Lily and Melissande, even Ladies Emma and Aurelia at the agency, did not even mention Ellen Clarkson's murder. Something that was hard to do as the story was splashed all over the newspapers.

The tension finally broke when a woman arrived at the agency claiming she needed my personal assistance. As soon as the door to my private office closed, she flat out asked me how I felt about being engaged to a murderer.

Enraged, I threw open my door and yelled, "Out!"

The woman jumped to her feet and confronted me. "If you think I won't stop asking questions, you're sadly mistaken."

"Get. Out!"

Lady Emma emerged from her office in a rush. "What's wrong?"

"This person is a newshound. She's not ever to cross our threshold again."

The reporter tossed her head. "You can't make me leave."

Betsy and Lady Emma each grabbed an arm, marched her out the door, and slammed it in her face.

Thankfully, there were no prospective clients in the reception area to watch that debacle.

Lady Aurelia must have heard the commotion because she came rushing down the steps just in time to witness the newshound's expulsion.

"The nerve of that woman!" Lady Emma said.

"I gather she asked an impertinent question in relation to the Oxford murder?" Lady Aurelia asked, interjecting an air of calmness into the highly charged atmosphere.

I blew out a breath to regain my composure. "She did."

"I was afraid that would happen. May I make a suggestion?" Lady Aurelia asked.

"Of course."

"Until this matter is settled, and the culprit is apprehended, there will be others who will darken our door with the same intent. We need to make you unapproachable."

"How?"

"I suggest you and I trade offices. If Lady Emma is amenable, she and I will handle the initial intake interviews. If we determine that a person has brought us an honest enquiry, we will consult you to determine who's to be assigned the case."

"Sounds like a great plan of action, Lady Aurelia," Lady Emma said.

"Thank you. But I have an additional suggestion. We can only protect you here. I expect you will be accosted in public settings as well. These newspaper hooligans do not have a proper bone in their bodies and will do anything to get a scoop. You will need to employ your disguises every time you step outside this door. Unfortunate, but necessary."

"You're right. I'll have Grace pack several, and I'll bring them with me tomorrow." I glanced down at my watch. "Now, ladies, I believe it's time for lunch, and I'm feeling a bit peckish. Italian, Indian, or something else?"

Ladies Emma and Aurelia exchanged glances and, in unison, cried out, "Pub fare."

"Fish and chips, it is!" I exclaimed.

* * *

Eager for things to return to normal, Mother decided to hold a supper party three days later with the usual family and close friends in attendance. Lady Emma and Lord Marlowe, Ned and Lady Lily, Lady Melissande and Lord Hollingsworth who'd returned from Oxford, Lord Rutledge and Lady Aurelia, and, of course, Robert, were all invited. With Father, Mother and me, the party made a perfect twelve.

The morning of the event I threw open my bedroom window and breathed in the air. It was cold, but not frigid. It was February, after all. And the winter sun sparkled brightly in a cloudless sky. With the promise of that perfect day, I felt everything would turn out right.

The morning editions of the London newspapers soon destroyed that illusion. Every blasted headline had taken aim at Robert. *Police Playing Favorites?*, one of them read. Another one declared *Scandal Brewing at the Met.* The worst was from *The Tell-All, A Murderer at Scotland Yard.* Robert had been tried and convicted by the press.

It was a somber crowd who gathered that evening for cocktails. Lord Rutledge appeared to be the most affected for his face held an alarming pallor. He'd always been slender, but he seemed to have lost weight. Not only that, but he also wasn't steady on his feet. Whereas before he'd employed a cane as an elegant accessory, tonight he leaned heavily on it to move about.

During a moment when Father claimed his attention, I pulled Robert aside. "Lord Rutledge seems to have grown quite infirm. Is he ill?"

The corners of his lips turned down. "His heart is failing."

"Oh, no."

"He's seeing a specialist on Harley Street. But—" He shook his head.

"Is there nothing that can be done?"

"He needs to rest, but he refuses to do so. And now, with everything that's going on—"

"—It makes things worse."

"Yes."

"Have you heard anything new about the murder investigation?"

He shook his head. "Scotland Yard has determined I best be kept ignorant of the enquiry."

I wanted to ask more questions, but just then Carlton stepped into the room to announce dinner. The meal was pleasant enough. While we enjoyed the beef tenderloin and Cabernet Sauvignon, we studiously ignored the subject uppermost in our minds. Mother wisely turned the discussion to the season, stating Ladies Lily and Melissande were bound to be its most favored debutantes.

Lily blushed while smiling softly at Ned. The season was

an opportunity for young ladies to find husbands, but her heart had already been given to my brother. At the end of the season, I expected their engagement would be announced.

Lady Melissande was in a similar situation. Her beau was the Duke of Andover who we'd met during a previous investigation. As he was busy strengthening diplomatic relations between his country and the British government, his visits were infrequent. Not only that, but his mother was recuperating from an earlier ordeal and was not venturing out in public. But he held the hope, as we all did, she'd be able to attend some of the social events. Until that happened, a full-blown courtship of Lady Melissande could not be conducted.

Once supper ended, the ladies withdrew to the drawing room while the gentlemen remained to drink port and smoke cigars. The peaceful interlude did not last long. A bare few minutes later, yelling erupted in the dining room.

"You can't just sit on your arse and wait to be charged. You must do something!"

"Oh, dear!" Mother said, worry apparent on her face.

"What's wrong?" Lady Melissande asked.

I came to my feet. "Lord Rutledge. He's angry at Robert." That outburst could only have been directed at him.

"Please, calm yourself, sir," Robert replied. "This upset is not good for your health."

"Don't you see? You're putting your entire future in danger." Lord Rutledge's voice was growing weaker. "You're placing everything in jeopardy."

The sound of a thud reached us.

"Sir! Lord Rutledge."

"Milord!"

All the ladies rushed into the dining room to find Lord Rutledge prostrate on the floor, his face a deadly shade of white, and Robert loosening his necktie.

Lord Rutledge had enough strength in him to whisper, "I can't die. Not until things are settled."

"Yes, sir." Robert retrieved a small notebook from his coat and handed it to Father. "If you could please telephone Doctor Goodman. His number is in there."

Father rushed out of the dining room toward the hallway where the nearest telephone was located.

"If you could bring Lord Rutledge to the drawing room," Mother said. "He can rest on one of the sofas while we await Doctor Goodman."

With Ned lending a hand, together they followed Mother's instructions. Once his mentor was resting comfortably, Robert knelt next to him.

Lord Rutledge's hand trembled against Robert's cheek. "My boy. My dear, dear boy." And then his eyelids fluttered closed.

"Oh, he's not? He didn't?" A clearly distraught Lady Lily asked.

"No," Robert said, head hanging down. "He still breathes."

We waited for what seemed like ages for Doctor Goodman to arrive. After bringing Lord Rutledge around, he gave him an elixir to drink. Within minutes, the medicine roused the marquis from his lethargy. "I want to go home."

"No, sir. You cannot," Doctor Goodman said before turning to Mother. "He should not be removed to his home. The shock to his heart would be too great."

"I'll have my housekeeper prepare a bedchamber for him," Mother said. "He can remain here as long as there's need."

"Sorry to be such an imposition, dear lady," Lord Rutledge said reaching out to her with a trembling hand.

"Nonsense," she said as she took it. "You're not an imposition but a dear friend. Now, if you'll excuse me, I'll go make the arrangements."

Once the room had been prepared, Robert and Ned

slowly carried Lord Rutledge up the stairs with Doctor Goodman bringing up the rear.

Upon Robert and Ned's return, the expressions on their faces spoke volumes about the seriousness of Lord Rutledge's condition. "He's resting now," Robert said. "Doctor Goodman is organizing a nurse to stay with him through the night. Another will arrive in the morning. They'll know what to do."

Threading my hand through his, I murmured, "I'm so sorry, Robert. I know how much you care for him."

He simply nodded. His emotions would allow him no more.

Once the nurse arrived and Doctor Goodman had given her care instructions, he returned downstairs to provide us with his report. "As you can see, Lord Rutledge is not well. He needs to rest; otherwise his heart might . . . " The rest of the words hung in the air. But he didn't need to finish. We all knew.

"Yes," Robert said.

Doctor Goodman handed Mother a note. "These are the things he's allowed to eat. No salt, no spices, definitely no smoking or spirits."

"We'll take the best care of him."

Once the doctor left, the other guests soon followed. Except, of course, the ones who resided with us and Lady Aurelia who'd been invited to stay the night.

Robert was the last to leave. I accompanied him to the foyer where he retrieved his outer garments. Sadly, he was too upset to banter. All he could do was whisper goodnight.

I climbed the stairs to my room where, to my surprise, I found a summons from Lord Rutledge.

"He wants to see you, Miss," my maid, Grace, said.

He was awake? Surely, the potion his physician had given

him would have encouraged sleep. But no matter. If Lord Rutledge needed to see me, see me he would. "Yes, of course."

I knocked softly on the door to his room. A tall woman with a no-nonsense air about her greeted me. "He wouldn't sleep until he saw you," she offered by way of explanation. "But please keep it brief. He needs his rest."

I nodded. "Lord Rutledge," I said once I reached the bed.

His eyes had been closed but he opened them when he heard my voice. "My dear Kitty. Thank you for coming."

"You're most welcome, milord. What do you wish of me?"

"I want you to investigate this murder."

My breath hitched. Should have known he would ask that of me. Unfortunately, it would not be an easy thing to do. "Robert—"

"I know he doesn't want you to. He's being a fool. He thinks they can't possibly accuse him because he's innocent. But you and I know they would. And more than likely, they will. I want you to make sure he doesn't pay for a crime he did not commit."

"I'll need to travel to Oxford. He'll notice my absence."

"Lie to him. It's the only way." Marshaling a strength he did not own, he captured my hand. "Promise me you'll investigate. Promise me."

"I promise." What else could I do? The man was too ill for me to gainsay him. "Now please get some rest, sir."

"Now I will." And with that, he closed his eyes and drifted off to sleep.

I, on the other hand, spent the rest of the night awake wondering how I would explain things to Robert.

CHAPTER 11

LIES AND DECEPTIONS

My first order of business was to devise a logical explanation for my absence. Together with Ladies Emma and Aurelia, we crafted a subterfuge.

It went something like this. Due to the notoriety of the Oxford matter and my connection to Robert, the agency was being besieged by members of the press who staged themselves outside our door waiting for me to appear. I couldn't very well remain closeted at home until the frenzy died down. The agency's caseload would not allow it. As luck would have it, a matter had come up which required travel to Birmingham. Hopefully, my absence would discourage the newshounds.

It was thin. More than likely, Robert would see through it in a minute. But I did not have time to hatch a cleverer ruse.

As I could not lie to Mother again, I told her the truth. She frowned about the deception but gave in when I explained Lord Rutledge had requested it of me. Rather than tell Robert in person, I telephoned him. Cowardly, I know. But if I presented myself to him, he would see through my lies. Once the travel plans had been arranged, I made the call.

"Birmingham, you say?" He inquired once I'd explained the details.

"Yes. I should be gone but a few days, a week at the most."

"Where will you be staying?"

"The Grand Hotel. It's right in the heart of the city."

"I know it well. You're not traveling alone?"

"Mister Clapham will accompany me." Actually, Hollingsworth would. I'd contacted him earlier that day. Once I explained the plan, he'd readily agreed to escort me to Oxford. Robert might not acknowledge the peril he was in, but Hollingsworth did. He wanted to do everything he could to ensure his friend was not blamed for Ellen Clarkson's murder. As before, he would reside at Lord Salverton's address while I conducted the investigation.

The next morning, we took the train to Oxford where Margaret was expecting us. When I'd telephoned her, I'd asked her to arrange an interview with Ellen Clarkson's younger brother, Oliver. I was pleased to learn she'd been able to do so.

"He will see you tomorrow at ten at his home."

"Did he balk at the request?" If he had, I needed to be prepared to overcome his objections.

"On the contrary. He was quite amenable to it," Margaret explained. "He's eager to get to the truth of his sister's murder."

"Any rumors spreading through the city?" I had to know the lay of the land before I ventured into Oxford.

She grinned. "Oh, yes. It's all anyone can talk about. Academics are quite the gossiping sort, you know. They thrive on scandals. When not applying themselves to their studies, that is."

"What are they saying?"

"Some think Robert was responsible, of course. But that's only to be expected given the testimony at the inquest. Others think she was accosted by a fiend, something along the lines of Jack the Ripper."

"But she wasn't mutilated like his victims were."

"That doesn't stop them from voicing that theory."

"What else?"

"Whoever seduced her."

"They don't think it was Robert? He wouldn't do such a thing."

"Those that knew him best agree with you. They know him for an honorable man." Before he entered Oxford, he'd saved the life of Lord Rutledge, suffering grievous injuries while doing so. "By all accounts, he was brilliant in his studies," Margaret continued. "Got a first in jurisprudence at Magdalen College, apparently. And he was not the sort to venture into the local pubs and get blind drunk night after night."

"As I did," Hollingsworth said.

"Did you really?" Margaret spouted in a curious tone.

"Oh, yes. I was thumbing my nose at Father. A useless endeavor as he couldn't have cared less. Many a night Robert had to pour me into my bed. As you can see, I've put away my childish ways."

"Good on you," Margaret offered with a soft smile.

"What do people say about the broken engagement?"

"Those who knew Robert believe what he said, that it was a mutual decision." She came to her feet. "But enough talk, our luncheon is waiting to be served, and I, for one, am starving."

"Me too," I said, linking arms with her and Hollingsworth.

After the meal, he took his leave, but not before Margaret exacted a promise he would join us for supper the next day along with Salverton. By then, Sebastian would be back in Oxford. He'd been tending to matters related to the upcoming growing season at Wynchcombe Castle. Thankfully, his estate manager, Jack Seward, had decided to remain at his employ, rather than resign, something we'd wondered about after the sad events surrounding Margaret and Sebastian's wedding.

The following morning, with the help of Margaret's maid, I dressed in my professional best. I'd opted not to bring Grace, as I felt the fewer people who knew what I was up to the better. I'd involved enough people in my lies. I didn't want to embroil her as well. Besides, my needs would not be onerous. Most of my time at Oxford, I would wear morning and afternoon dresses, although I had packed two evening gowns for those occasions that called for it. I had no need of someone to style my coiffure as I wore my hair in a bob. All I required was someone to button me up and polish my footwear. And that Margaret's maid could handle, as my sister herself had stated.

I arrived at the Clarkson residence promptly at ten where I was politely welcomed by Oliver Clarkson. A young man of about twenty-four years of age, tall, dark-haired and dark-eyed, he had an air of solemnity about him as he held a book to his chest.

"Thank you for agreeing to talk to me, Mister Clarkson."

"I'm glad to do so, Miss Worthington. I want to find the truth about my sister's death. If you can do that, I will be forever in your debt. I've asked for tea to be served."

"Thank you."

While we waited for the tea to be brought, I praised his home. "It's a lovely room."

"Thank you, but I can't take credit for it. My mother decorated it."

"She had excellent taste."

"That she did." A fond smile bloomed across her lips. "I wanted to leave it as it was."

"I understand."

"I've rarely lived here, you know," he said with an almost guilty expression on his face.

Well, that was interesting. "Really? How is that so?"

"Well, from the time I was eight to age seventeen, I was away at boarding school. After Father passed away, I resided with Professor Burgess during the holidays. He was gracious enough to offer me his home while I attended Oxford as well. He thought I would just rattle about this place."

"I see."

The maid entered with the tea service. While she poured cups for us, we turned to rather desultory conversation. Once we'd refreshed ourselves, he rested his saucer on the small table next to him. "Now what do you wish to ask of me?"

I fetched a notebook from my handbag. "Do you mind if I take notes? I find it helps me recall things." At the beginning of every investigation, I always started a new one. I'd already made quite a few notations in this one, mainly the information I'd learned at the inquest and what Robert had shared.

"No. I prefer it in fact."

"I'd like to start with you, Mister Clarkson. Could you tell me something about yourself?" Most people felt comfortable talking about themselves. It was a fairly easy way to begin a discussion before asking the more difficult questions.

"Aaah. Let's see, well, I'm a research fellow in the Department of Astronomy. I loved looking at the stars as a lad."

"How wonderful. I understand you were away at school the year your sister became engaged?"

"I was fourteen at the time. I studied day and night. I wanted Father to be proud of me, you see."

"I'm sure he was. Did you come home for the Christmas holiday?"

"Yes. That's when I met Robert Crawford, Ellen's fiancé. He seemed a nice enough chap. I paid little attention to them as I was busy with my studies."

"Even during the holiday?"

"My father instilled a love of learning in me, Miss Worthington. As you can see"—he pointed to the tome he'd rested on the small table—"I'm rarely without a book in my hand."

"You're like my sister. She loves learning as well."

He cracked a small smile. The first time he'd done that. It transformed his whole face from ordinary to downright handsome. "Yes, I know. She's well known in Oxford for her devotion to her studies."

"Was your father pleased with their engagement?"

"He was ecstatic. Father looked very favorably upon Mister Crawford, felt he would make Ellen an excellent husband. And, of course, Ellen's future would be settled."

"That was important to him?"

"Yes. Her engagement to his favorite pupil meant he need not worry about her. Mister Crawford would take good care of Ellen. His means were modest at that time, but Father thought he had a promising future. Her dowry would ensure they had an excellent start to their married life."

"Do you know if her dowry was contingent upon her marriage?"

"Or until she turned twenty-five. Those were the conditions. But, of course, that was not a problem. Ellen was very happy about her engagement. She was always smiling around him. They got on very well."

"But then once your father passed away, things changed."

"Yes." His smile vanished. "I was home for the summer, although I was not in the house when Father's heart failed. I was out with my mates. I returned to the cries of Ellen's wailing. It was a horrible sound. I hear it sometimes in my sleep."

Ten years gone and he still remembered it as it was yesteryear. "I'm so sorry for your loss, Mister Clarkson."

His emotions got the better of him, and he cast down his gaze. "Thank you."

I gave him some time to compose himself before asking, "After your father's passing, what did you do? Did you stay here or return to school?" Of course, I knew the answer from the inquest. But I wanted his take on it.

"I went to live with Professor Burgess for the two weeks left of my summer holiday."

"You didn't go to your aunt and uncle's as your sister did?"

"I was told it'd be best to stay with the professor as my sister was prostrate with grief. I had no complaint about my accommodation. Professor Burgess was very kind to me."

"Who informed you you'd be staying with Professor Burgess?"

"You know, I really can't recall. I was in rather a daze at the time. Someone packed my things, and Professor Burgess led me to his automobile—an Oxford two-seater. Brand new."

He'd been a boy, clearly interested in motorcars, so it stood to reason he remembered that. "Did you see your sister again?"

The corners of his mouth turned down. "No. I was told she was suffering from melancholia and best left to the kindness of my aunt and uncle."

How very odd. Brother and sister would find comfort in each other. And yet, they'd been kept apart.

"Do you know what happened to break off the engagement between Mister Crawford and your sister?"

"No. I only knew that it ended."

"Who told you?"

"Professor Burgess. He sent me the occasional letter at school. I was sad to hear it as Ellen had been so happy being engaged to him."

"Did she write you about her travel to Plymouth?"

"No. I heard about it much later. I sent a letter to my uncle inquiring about her welfare. He wrote back telling me she'd gone to Plymouth. I thought it was a strange thing for her to do. We didn't have many dealings with that branch of the family."

"Why was that?"

He shrugged. "Something had caused a rift between the two brothers. What it was I never knew."

"Why do you think she chose to do so?"

He looked off into the distance. "She would have felt shame about what happened to her."

"The seduction you mean?" Best put it as kindly as I could.

"Yes. If it got out, it would have caused a scandal. She wouldn't want that to happen, as it was bound to affect Aunt Imelda. She was very close to her. She'd taken on the role of mother after ours passed away. Ellen wouldn't have wanted to hurt her."

"And you never heard from your sister again?"

"No, I did not." A shadow of sadness passed over his face. "She used to send me packages in the post, once a month like clockwork, with long letters detailing the minutiae of her life. But after our father's death, they stopped coming." He glanced up. "I missed them. I miss her. She was a lovely sister to an awkward young chap."

CHAPTER 12

ELLEN'S BEDCHAMBER

To my surprise, Ellen's room had been kept intact. Apparently, her brother could not bring himself to donate her things to charities. By keeping it the way it'd been, it made him feel as though she was still there.

Ellen's death was not the only tribulation in the family. Oliver Clarkson was suffering, and so was Mister Staunton and Reverend Clarkson. What a tragedy the whole thing had been and continued to be.

I examined the room as methodically as I could. Of course, the police had been through it. I imagined they must have taken quite a few items. Her bed, with its iron frame, had been immaculately preserved which must have been difficult. Everything about it was white from the spread to her pillows to the bed skirt.

The clothes in the wardrobe were very feminine in nature. But they'd been styled for a girl, not a woman of twenty-one years in age. How very odd. I searched for a diary, but I didn't find it. If she'd had one, she would taken it with her when she'd moved in with her aunt and uncle. Or the police could have confiscated it as evidence. Either way, it wasn't here. Oliver had suggested I talk to his sister's friends—Letitia Fairbright, now a lecturer of English and history at St. Hilda's College, and Mrs. Dorothy Swanson, married to an Oxford Balliol College Professor. Maybe they'd know something about it. Or maybe he would.

Her vanity table contained a silver brush and comb set, a framed picture of her father, another one of a woman, more than likely her mother, and one of a younger version of Oliver Clarkson. There was one of a young woman, tall and slender, close in coloring to Oliver. And, I realized, me. Could it possibly be Ellen herself? Is that why Robert was attracted to me? Because I resembled his lost love? I shook off those thoughts as they would be of little help and moved on to the other items. A stylish perfume bottle had once been filled with attar of roses. The same fragrance I used.

I gritted my teeth and carried on. The drawers on the right side of the vanity held items related to the household—weekly menus, lists of items to be purchased as well as past expenditures, and matters she wished to discuss with her father. She'd been very methodical about it. On the left, she kept ribbons, hair pins. But, other than a container of face powder, she hadn't owned any maquillage products. But then, she'd had no need. If the photograph was anything to go by, she'd been a natural beauty. I swallowed hard as I recalled the variety of items on my vanity table. Lipstick, blush, mascara, and more. I owned them all.

The contents of the bottom drawer were a surprise. And yet, ones I should have expected. Letters from Robert postmarked the summer of 1913. How odd the police hadn't taken them. I debated whether to read them. There were bound to be personal in nature. But how could I not? I needed to know the truth.

There were twelve of them, one for every week they were separated. I smiled to myself. He would be methodical about his letter writing. It was easy to tell the ones that were written prior to her father's death. They were filled with the minutiae of his life. The daily police rounds, descriptions of his parents, the occasional evening out with his mates. He ended them with 'All my love, Robert'. I took a deep breath and dived into the ones he'd penned after the funeral. Whereas the earlier ones had been light in nature, these were filled with regret. The fact he wasn't there to comfort her gnawed at him. That was clear from his words. Although his correspondence was constant as he posted a letter every week, apparently Ellen had not been. There were gentle reminders he hadn't heard from her for over two weeks, three weeks. And then there was one that was a cry from the heart. 'I haven't abandoned you, Ellie. I love you as much as I ever have." That was the last one he sent. It was posted in late September just before he returned to Oxford.

Finished reading them, I tucked them back in the drawer, gently closed it, and wiped the tears from my face. Watching my reflection in Ellen's mirror, I brushed my hair, repaired my makeup, freshened up my lipstick. Only then did I go in search of Oliver Clarkson.

"May I borrow this photograph of Ellen? It will prove helpful when we ask questions about her."

"Yes, you may. I will want it back, though."

"Of course. Once we're done with the investigation, I will return it. Do you know if Ellen kept a diary? Most young women do."

"She did. The police searched for it, and so did I. But we never found it."

Finding that diary rose to the top of my list. It would not only provide clues as to Ellen's state of mind but a narrative of her last days on earth. Whatever it took, I had to find it.

CHAPTER 13

SUPPER AT THE WYNCHCOMBES'

"How did it go?" Margaret asked as soon as I returned.

"Oliver Clarkson was very accommodating. He answered all my questions and even allowed me to inspect his sister's room."

"Did you discover anything important?"

Rather than answer that question, I spoke about something that troubled me. "He and Ellen were kept apart after their father's death, supposedly because she was suffering from melancholia."

Her brow scrunched. "You learned that at the inquest."

"Yes, but it's bothered me since."

"Why?"

"From all accounts, both loved their father dearly. Wouldn't it have been better if they had the opportunity to console each other? That's what we did after Emily died. I don't know what I would have done without you."

"We are sisters, close in age. They were of opposite sexes, seven years apart. It was not the same."

"Yes, there is that. Still . . .?"

"Yes?"

"I can't help but think there is more to it. I didn't find the answer to that riddle, though."

She pressed my hands. "You'll figure it out. You always do. What about Ellen's room?"

"Much to my surprise, he'd kept the room intact. Everything was as if she'd just left. It was rather eerie."

"What do you mean?"

"I felt like her ghost was hovering over me."

My sister, ever the pragmatist, hitched a doubting brow.

Clearly, it was time to put aside my fanciful musings. "Anyway, the room was so well preserved, I was able to gain an understanding of her life. She functioned as her father's housekeeper. There was clear evidence of that. She kept lists of items to be purchased, both for the household and for meals. I also found weekly menus dating back to the beginning of the summer. Notations on them indicated she'd consulted their cook, as she'd scratched out some of the items. She seemed very conscious of not repeating the same dish. And then there was the young woman side of her life. A silver brush and comb set, perfume, hair ribbons. A white spread on her bed. And Robert's letters. The ones he wrote to her when he was away at London that summer."

"Did you read them?"

I hitched up my chin. "I had to. I need to gain an understanding of their relationship. But something struck me as odd."

"What?"

"The fact they were there. You would think the police would've taken them away."

"Maybe they didn't reveal anything important."

"They didn't." I glanced down to fiddle with my fingers. "It was rather disturbing reading love letters from my fiancé to another woman."

"Yes, I expect it would be." Her tone was pure kindness itself.

A clamor from the foyer reached us, and she jumped to her feet, joy filling her face. "Sebastian's home."

She flew out the door toward the man she married. I followed in time to see his arms close around her. Not wanting to intrude on their intimate embrace, I turned away.

But Sebastian had spotted me. "Kitty!"

"Hello."

He embraced me as well before holding me at arms' length so he could study me. "How are you?"

"Fine."

His concerned expression revealed my word for a lie. "Up to your elbows in your investigation, I gather."

"Yes."

"I want to hear all about it. Later, though. Right now, I'd like a wash and a change of clothes. It was a beastly train ride."

Margaret threaded her arm through his. "Everything's waiting for you upstairs." She turned to me. "We'll see you before supper. Cocktails at eight. Hollingsworth and Salverton will be here. Oh, and our next-door neighbor, Lady Rawlston, and her daughter, Lady Delphine." And then she and Sebastian climbed the stairs, their arms around each other's waists.

It was not only a wash and a change of clothes that would occupy their time, for supper was a couple of hours away. But who was I to decry them their happiness? Even if I was about as miserable as could be.

* * *

THAT EVENING, we gathered for supper along with Lord Salverton, Hollingsworth's friend who turned out to be rather tall, powerfully built, and handsome in the bargain. Lady Rawlston, who'd arrived fifteen minutes early with her daughter, Lady Delphine in tow, was definitely a mother on the prowl. Lady Delphine, you see, was unmarried. Her mother knew a golden opportunity when she saw one. And two unattached, titled bachelors most certainly qualified.

Lady Rawlston and her daughter were a study in contrast. While the mother never ceased talking, Lady Delphine barely breathed a word. While Lady Rawlston's neck, hands, and bosom, were heavily adorned with jewels, the only decoration Lady Delphine wore was a necklace composed of perfectly matched pearls. Lady Rawlston's coiffure, with its wigs and pastiches that resembled Georgian fashion of old, was in danger of toppling over. Her daughter, adopting the style of present day, wore her hair in a simple bob, with only a hair ribbon that matched her dress. And what a dress it was! I would need to find out the name of her modiste. The style was very modern, made of silk, low waisted with a pleated skirt, a rosette high on one shoulder. The shade, an azalea pink, was perfectly suited to her coloring, as she was a blonde. Not only that, it brought out the blue in her eyes.

"I love your gown, Lady Delphine," I said after supper when we were seated in the drawing room. "The style is so *au courant*." Before supper, Margaret had given me a rundown on her next-door neighbors. Apparently, they'd recently traveled to Paris to refresh their wardrobes.

She pinked up. "Oh, thank you."

"Is it Parisian?"

"In a manner of speaking."

A strange answer to be sure.

"Is it a Worth?" It didn't appear to be so, but then maybe they'd changed their spring styles.

"No. It's a new modiste."

I was bound and determined to get the name, if for no other reason than I could share it with Angelique, my own designer. Surely, she'd know all about this new talent. But before I could inquire further, the gentlemen joined us.

That's when Lady Rawlston pounced. "Oh, Lord Salverton, a little birdie told me you were part of the Oxford Rowing team."

"Yes, ma'am. Both 1912 and 1913, don't you know?" He flashed her a charming smile.

"How very clever of you."

What rowing had to do with cleverness, I had no idea.

"Five of us competed at the 1912 Summer Olympics in Stockholm, took the Gold in the eights, by Jove. You recall, Hollingsworth?"

"Yes. It was a glorious win."

"Do you still row?"

"Oh, no. Much too busy with my stamp collection."

Lady Rawlston blinked several times. "I beg your pardon."

"Quite valuable, if I say so myself. I am on the hunt for the British Guiana 1 cent Magenta, the rarest stamp in the world."

If Lord Salverton thought that would deter Lady Rawlston from further enquiries, he was sadly mistaken. She was desperate to find a titled husband for her daughter, and he more than fit the bill. "Lady Salverton must be very pleased with your accomplishments."

"My mother certainly was. Sadly, she passed on to her glory several years ago. Only a few months after my papa. She was quite devoted to him, you know."

"How sad. So, there's no current Lady Salverton?" The lady simply did not give up.

"No. Nor is there likely to be."

"Oh?"

"I've been cursed, you see."

"Cursed, sir?"

"Too much blunt."

"Blunt? Money, you mean?"

"Exactly. I'm too rich. When you add brains, brawn, and breeding. Well, you see my predicament."

More furious blinking on Lady Rawlston's part. "No, sir. I'm afraid I don't."

"I'm too much man. No woman could ever hope to measure up to my magnificence. So sadly, I'm doomed to walk this earth alone."

"But, sir—"

"No, no. there's no sense in arguing. My mind is made up."

Trying not to laugh, I bit down on my lip. Margaret had to turn away. Sebastian had no such compunction. He was wildly grinning at Salverton's elusive maneuvers.

Giving up on Salverton, Lady Rawlston turned to Hollingsworth. "What about you, sir?"

"Confirmed bachelor, I'm afraid. I'm an explorer, you see. I can't expect any lady to suffer while I sail the seven seas. I'm often gone for years at a time."

"But sir, the lady wouldn't suffer. She can find a myriad of ways to entertain herself."

"Not while she was wearing a chastity belt, she wouldn't," Hollingsworth deadpanned.

Lady Rawlston stiffened in outrage. "I beg your pardon. That's positively medieval."

"My point exactly. I wouldn't want to enforce such suffering on anyone."

I didn't know who was more outrageous. No wonder they got along so well.

Having failed at her quest, Lady Rawlston soon took her leave, with her daughter trailing in her wake.

The rest of the evening proceeded quite enjoyably. But all good things, sooner or later, must come to an end. While saying goodbye to Lord Salverton, I said. "It was a pleasure meeting you, milord. I was quite in the dumps today, but your wit cheered me up no end."

He bowed over my hand, looked me straight in the eye. "Don't lose courage, dear lady. Faint hearts never won a war. And 'tis a war you're engaged in."

"Yes, I do fear so."

"If I can be of service, all you need do is telephone."

"Thank you. I shall keep that in mind."

He nodded in approval before turning to his friend. "Coming, Hollingsworth?"

"In a minute."

"I'll go fire up old Minnie then." He bowed his head once more, and then he was gone.

When Hollingsworth approached me, all I could think to say was "Who's Minnie"?

"His motorcar."

I couldn't help but smile. "He's quite unique, your friend."

"You don't know the half of it. But don't let all his blather fool you. He has a razor-sharp mind." He turned serious once more. "Will you be all right?"

"I believe so." When he raised a doubting brow, I said. "I hope so, anyway."

"Is there anything you wish me to do?"

"For the moment, talk to people around Oxford. I need to know what they're thinking."

"It's bound to be quite nasty."

"I expect so. There might be a kernel or two of truth out there, however."

"Very well. I'll stick to my task and report. What will you do?"

"Talk to a couple of Ellen's friends. They might know something." Or at least I hoped they did.

CHAPTER 14

A VISIT WITH MRS. SWANSON

Mrs. Swanson graciously welcomed me the next afternoon. In her early thirties and blonde, she eschewed the latest bob styles and kept her hair long and pinned back in a bun. She was also quite visibly pregnant.

Once we'd gotten the ubiquitous offer of tea out of the way, I observed the niceties.

"You have a beautiful home, Mrs. Swanson." Not as impressive as Margaret's but still it was a lovely two-story structure with impressive wainscoting. The furniture seemed to hail from Victorian times, although she was not one to overcrowd her home with furniture. Her judicious use of plants and flowers gave the place a warm, homey feel.

"Thank you." She folded her hands over her burgeoning belly. "Oliver Clarkson's note stated you wished to discuss my friendship with his sister."

"If you wouldn't mind."

"Not at all. But I am curious, Miss Worthington. What is your interest in this matter?"

So, Oliver Clarkson had not revealed my connection to the case. Since I believed whenever possible, honesty was the best policy, I told her the truth. "I'm engaged to Robert Crawford."

"Ahh, I see. Things are looking rather grim for him."

I said nothing, as I didn't wish to expound on that thought. "I want to find out the truth."

"Even if the truth doesn't lead where you wish?"

"Yes."

"Very well, but I must caution you. As you can see, I'm in expectation of a happy event. Nature sometimes proves rather inconvenient, so I may have to cut our discussion short."

In other words, if I asked a question she didn't wish to answer, she would use that excuse. "Of course. I understand."

I seemed to have overcome her reluctance, because she leaned back into her seat and relaxed her pose. "Well, then, feel free to ask me anything."

I fetched my journal from my handbag. "You don't mind if I take notes. It helps to recall statements."

"No. Please do."

"Thank you. Now if you could tell me when you first met Ellen."

"Let's see. It must have been 1899. We both attended the Brewster Academy for Young Ladies. She'd been taught by a governess before that. But when her mother passed, her father felt it best if she were sent to boarding school."

"How old was she?"

"Eight?"

"Did she enjoy the academy?"

"No. She was miserable. Understandable, given the circumstances. She'd adored her mother. But when she died in childbirth, her father felt he could not cope with an eight-year-old and a brand-new babe. As time passed, she grew used to it, but she never enjoyed it. She was an average student who obtained passable grades." There was an air of superiority to Mrs. Swanson. Clearly, she thought herself a better person than Ellen.

"How long was she there?"

"Until she graduated. She must have been sixteen at the time. She returned to Oxford where she set about keeping house for her father. Something she rather enjoyed as I understand."

"You remained friends?"

"We were not bosom bows, more friendly than friend. Letitia Fairbright was much closer to her. They shared a room, you see."

I jotted that down in my journal.

"Did she socialize much after she graduated?"

"Not at all."

"Really?"

"Yes. That's why we weren't especially close. Young ladies and gentlemen of our class regularly attended balls, suppers, picnics around Oxford. But Ellen was never allowed to join us. Professor Clarkson was quite strict with her. He felt the Oxford crowd was too wild and wanted to preserve her innocence. Rather sad, seeing what came out at the trial. Do you think it's true?"

"I have no idea, Mrs. Swanson. It will be a particularly difficult matter to prove."

"Yes. Still, it gives you pause."

"So how did she become engaged to Robert, to Mister Crawford? Do you know?"

"Oh, yes. Oxford is in many ways a small town. If somebody sneezes, we soon find out about it. Mister Crawford's courtship of Ellen was well-known in my social circle. Many of them attended Oxford, you see. Professor Clarkson always invited his most promising students to his home, and Mister Crawford—well, he certainly was that. Brilliant, my husband called him."

"Oh, did your husband and Robert attend Oxford at the same time?"

She let out a tittering laugh. "Oh, no. William was not a student. He was a lecturer back then. Taught Mister Crawford in one subject or another. Can't recall which one. He's now a professor." Suddenly, she twinged.

"Are you all right?"

"Just the babe making himself known."

"You're hoping for a male child?"

"After three girls, he better be." She put a hand to the small of her back. "If we could hurry this along, I'd appreciate it."

"Of course." I glanced at my notes to determine what were the most important questions. "So Miss Clarkson and Mister Crawford got engaged?"

"Yes. In the, let me think, the autumn of 1912. She was instantly smitten with him, and, by all accounts, he with her. A marriage made in heaven, her father was fond of saying. So, when they got engaged, everyone was happy. Ellen, of course, was thrilled she was going to get a family and a household of her own."

"But then they broke off the engagement. Do you know why?"

"Well, rumor had it he'd given her the heave-ho. While in London, he'd met someone more suitable to his ambitions within the police department. Since neither Professor Clarkson, nor Ellen, had any connections to that world, he'd be better off with this mystery woman."

"But you didn't believe it?"

"No. He wouldn't have done such a thing. From all accounts, he was too honorable for that."

"How do you know he was honorable?"

"He never lifted any skirts, and heaven knows there were plenty of women, from barmaids to gentle ladies of breeding, who tossed themselves at him. As far as I knew the only woman in his life was Ellen. But, of course, I was not aware of anything that happened while he was in London." She shifted in her seat as if she was uncomfortable. "Anything else?"

"Only one more question. Did you see her after she broke off her engagement?"

"I paid her a condolence call after her father's death. And again, after I heard the news about the breakup of her engagement. She was devastated. A week or two later, she left for Plymouth. We didn't correspond, and I never saw her again."

I arrived at Margaret's home to find a letter from Robert. "I'm staying at the Prince of Wales. Same room as before. Come see me tomorrow at ten."

I hadn't fooled him for a minute.

CHAPTER 15

ROBERT AT OXFORD

It took but a brief knock on the door to his hotel room door for it to fly open. If I had any expectation of conducting a calm, logical discussion, I put paid to that notion after one glance at him. Going by his flared nostrils and flinty gaze, he was furious with me.

Still, I put on a brave face as I advanced into the chamber, "Good morning, Robert."

He did not return the greeting but simply shut the door before facing me. "You said you were traveling to Birmingham to conduct an investigation, and yet here you are in Oxford. You lied to me."

"You forbade me from making enquiries into the murder of Ellen Clarkson. What was I to do?"

"Obey me." His quiet tone held an undertone of repressed anger.

"Obey you? You promised when we got engaged you

would never make demands of me, and yet that's exactly what you're doing. Sir, you do not command my behavior. All you can do is suggest." I took a deep breath, released it. Yelling at each other would never solve anything. Robert was a logical man. He could be swayed with a rational argument. "I've solved other murders before, you know."

But he would not be swayed. "That was different."

"How, Robert?"

"Those matters did not involve me, my past, my engagement to a woman I loved. I loved her, Kitty. Can you come to terms with that?" He towered over me, his eyes blazing with a fire I'd never seen before.

"I already have." Most certainly a lie, but I was not about to reveal the state of my distress. "I knew you were once engaged."

"How?"

"Mother accidentally overheard a conversation between you and Lord Rutledge at a supper at his home."

"You never asked me about it."

"I was dissuaded from doing so by Mother. She felt it would be best to wait until you brought it up. You never did." Which hurt even more than learning about the engagement.

His gaze narrowed. "Did you discuss the subject with someone else?"

"Hollingsworth. He knew you during your days at Oxford. I figured he'd know."

"And what did he say?"

"That I should discuss it with you."

"You never did."

"No. I followed Mother's advice." I challenged him. "You should have told me. I deserved to know."

"And what could I have told you?"

"That you were engaged once. See? That's not so hard."

"And you would have been satisfied with that simple answer?"

When I did not respond, he said, "No, you wouldn't have. You would have asked for book, chapter, and verse."

"Give me more credit than that, if you please." A small smile curved my lip. "I would have been satisfied with book and chapter."

He approached me, all the anger leached out of him. He curved his hand around my cheek. "Catherine, it will be difficult for you to remain objective. That could lead to mistakes."

"Probably so, but don't you see? I can't just sit at home waiting for the axe to fall."

He barked out a laugh. "They don't execute people with axes, anymore, my darling. They hang them."

Suddenly, tears started. Leaning against his chest, I allowed them to fall. "Please don't joke about it. I can't bear it."

"Don't cry for me. I don't deserve them after acting like a brute."

I hitched up my chin. "I'll determine when and why to shed my tears, sir. And if I determine you're worth them, then I shall."

"Such a fierce spirit. Have I told you lately that I love you?"

"No." I sniffed.

"Well, I do, even when you don't follow my wishes." He captured my hands with his. "Catherine, I don't wish you to get hurt. And it's bound to get particularly onerous, especially after today."

I swiped away the moisture on my cheeks. "What do you mean after today?"

"I've been summoned by Inspector Gordon of the Oxford Constabulary. He wants to talk to me."

The sinking feeling in my stomach landed with a thud. "Interrogate you, you mean?"

"It doesn't rise to that level, but for all intent and purpose, yes."

"You will have a solicitor present?"

"Of course. So no need to worry."

"You will tell me how it went."

He shook his head. "Best not."

"Why?"

"His questions and my answers are bound to upset you. That's the last thing I wish. And there are some matters I wish to keep private." Before I had a chance to object, he continued, "Yes, even from you."

"But how am I to investigate if I don't know what you tell him?"

"You'll figure it out. You always do."

He held secrets about what happened back then. Secrets he didn't want me to know. But it'd be my job to find out. If he wouldn't talk, maybe another would. "May I talk to Hollingsworth about Ellen?"

"He barely knew her."

"Even so, I'd like his take."

"Very well if you must." He bracketed my shoulders. "My darling. There's a murderer out there. He's killed once. He'll kill again. Be careful."

"I will."

But we both knew I couldn't control everything. All I could do was my best.

"If your investigation calls for you to travel somewhere, have Hollingsworth accompany you."

"I will. At the moment, he's feeling out the town. See what he can pick up. He and Lord Salverton."

"Salverton? How did he get involved?"

"Hollingsworth is staying at his home. He came to supper at Margaret and Sebastian's a couple of nights ago. Why? Is there something I should know about him?"

"He's not what he seems."

"You warned me off Hollingsworth once. Turned out you were best mates. Is this more of the same?"

"No. I never knew Salverton. We ran with different crowds."

"Then why the warning?"

"Just keep away from him. Whatever you do, don't get him involved in your enquiries."

He already was, but I wasn't about to reveal that to Robert. "When's your appointment with Inspector Gordon?" I asked.

"Two o'clock. We have time to enjoy a luncheon. I'd prefer to stay in the room. Reporters are bound to be outside."

"I prefer it as well." I treasured every moment I spent with Robert.

At the end of the meal, he took my hands into his and kissed them. "I love you, Catherine."

"I know." I grinned.

"But we can't talk anymore."

My breath hitched. "Wh-what do you mean?"

"My darling. We're not married. Our discussions are not confidential. Inspector Gordon can haul you into the constabulary and question you. I don't want you to go through that."

I tossed my head. "Well, if he does, I'll refuse to answer."

"Which will make me appear guilty."

My breath hitched. I wanted to challenge him, but I didn't. "It will be hell." There was hardly that went by that we didn't see each other or talk on the telephone.

"I know. I'm so sorry." His gaze held nothing but kindness.

Desperate for a light in the darkness, I said, "Tell me it will be all right."

"It will be all right."

But I could tell he was lying.

CHAPTER 16

A CONVERSATION IN A GARDEN

After the meeting with Robert, I needed to regain my bearings. So I decided to wander through Margaret's back garden. It was a rare fine winter day filled with sunshine with nary a cloud in the sky. As long as I wore my coat, a scarf, and a wool hat, I would be warm enough. It turned out Lady Delphine had the same idea.

Meaning just to say hello, I greeted her, but she smiled and waved me over. As ignoring her request would be extremely rude, I stepped through the gate that separated the properties and joined her on the other side.

"I really don't mean to interrupt, Miss Worthington. If you wish to enjoy your solitude, I'll be glad to cease my attentions."

"Oh, no. It's fine. I was just clearing my head."

"You must have a lot on your mind."

"Yes," was all I could say. I couldn't share my worries with her.

Thankfully, she took the conversation in another direction. "Your sister seems to enjoy her studies."

I smiled. "Margaret was a born scholar. She's the brightest of my siblings. Well, she and my oldest brother, Ned. He has quite a head for business."

"Are there more siblings?"

"Two brothers, but only one sister. There was one other, Emily. She succumbed to the Spanish influenza."

"How sad."

"Yes, it was rather. What about you?"

"I'm the lone offspring which explains my mother's ambitions for me. She wishes her only child to shine in society, even though I have no desire to do so."

"Oh?"

"I've suffered through three seasons, Miss Worthington, and Mother is determined to put me through a fourth. I've refused to do so. That was the impetus for Mother's behavior last night. She wishes to see me wed to a lord of the realm."

"Oh, I understand, believe me."

"Yes, but your season was a great success."

"You were there?" Embarrassment filled me. Of course, she'd been there. She just said she'd gone through three seasons. "I beg your pardon. Of course, you were."

"Don't apologize. It was no wonder you did not notice me. I was in hiding behind the biggest potted plants I could find."

"Heavens! You're just like Margaret then. She didn't give two figs during her season. Spent most of her time hiding in corners. Reading books, if you can imagine. If any gentleman had the audacity to ask her to dance, she trod on every one of his toes."

"She didn't wish to snag a husband then?"

"She did not. Her dream was to attend Oxford. So she crafted a proposal which Mother reluctantly accepted. If she didn't 'take', she would be allowed to matriculate at the university. As you can see, she succeeded."

"And yet she managed to snag a duke."

"He wasn't a duke then, only the heir. And she couldn't have cared less for the title, only for Sebastian."

She sighed deeply. "I wish I could be like her, or you. But I'm afraid Mama will not allow what I want to do."

"What do you desire?"

"I want to open my own modiste establishment. Please don't laugh."

"Why would I laugh? You obviously have excellent taste going by last night's frock and what you're wearing now."

Moving closer, she whispered. "Don't tell anyone, but I made them both."

"Did you really? You're very talented. You will need funds, though, to open your own shop." Her father certainly had the money, successful businessman that he was. But would he approve of her scheme? "How does your father feel about this endeavor? Have you discussed it with him?"

"I have. He's willing to foot the bill, as long as I get Mama's approval, which of course she refuses to give." She sighed. "I'll never achieve my dream."

"What if you negotiate terms with Lady Rawlston?"

"What do you mean?"

"Well, your Mama wishes you to attend another season. Tell her you'll do so. If by the end of the season, you don't obtain a respectable proposal from a peer, you'll be allowed to open your own salon."

"But what if I do receive an offer of marriage?"

"Talk to Margaret. She'll give you pointers on how to avoid that dreadful fate." Margaret's stratagems had been to make herself as unappealing as possible to each gentleman. Before the season got started, she'd made a list of all the eligible gentlemen and researched their likes and dislikes. If a gentleman loved horses, she hated them. If he preferred the country, she'd say she could never live away from the city. If a gentleman was counting on her to become a broodmare, she'd drum up a female complaint that made it nigh impossible for her to have children. The key was to match the unfavorable trait to every gentleman. As organized as Margaret was, I was sure she still had that list somewhere. It would need to be updated since that was compiled three seasons ago. But it would give Lady Delphine a foundation.

She laughed. "Oh, Miss Worthington, I'm so glad I ran into you." She stood in a hurry. "You don't mind if I dash off? Mama will be home in half an hour, and I want to marshal my thoughts so I can present the proposal tonight."

"Best do it in the morning after breakfast. People are more amenable at that time. Trust me, I know."

"Very well." As I came to my feet, she hugged me. "Wish me luck."

"Good luck." I pressed her hands. "I have a good feeling about this."

And with that she was off in a much lighter frame of mind than when I'd first seen her.

During the season, Lady Delphine would need to tread a very fine line between being approachable and evasive. Her mother would certainly insist on the former. I didn't think her mother would refuse the proposal, though. She was so eager to see her daughter wed, she would agree to the scheme. It would make for an entertaining season, that was for sure.

"Kitty!" Margaret's voice hailed me from her back door. "A letter just arrived in the afternoon post. I think it's the one you were expecting."

CHAPTER 17

HOLLINGSWORTH'S REVELATIONS

Indeed, it was. I'd written Reverend Clarkson, Ellen's cousin, requesting an audience with him. It was his letter that had come in the post. Thankfully, he agreed to see me the next day which meant I did not have a moment to lose as the journey to Plymouth would take the better part of a day.

The first order of business was to contact Hollingsworth as I would need an escort for the trip. Not only was he happy to do so, but he volunteered to make the travel arrangements. Once those were set, I sent Reverend Clarkson a telegram advising him of my time of arrival.

The next morning Hollingsworth and I boarded the train to London. At a little over one hour, that segment of our journey would be the shortest. At Paddington station, we climbed aboard the train to Plymouth for the five-hour ride. Hollingsworth had been clever enough to make a luncheon reservation on the restaurant car for which I was extremely grateful. Riddled with nerves as I was, I hadn't been able to enjoy much more than toast and coffee for breakfast. So by the time we boarded the Plymouth-bound train, my stomach was making its needs known.

Once we finished our meal, we returned to our compartment. With two hours to go before our arrival at Plymouth, I decided to broach a subject he'd been previously reluctant to discuss.

"Once before I brought up the subject of Robert's fiancée. You suggested I talk to him which I have now done. I would now like to learn your take on things."

"I suppose Robert has given his blessing."

"He has."

"Well, then, what do you wish to know?"

"Your impression of her, for starters."

He raised a brow but answered readily enough. "I did not know her as well as Robert did. Professor Clarkson only invited his students to dinner. I was purportedly studying anthropology. In reality, I was majoring in drunkenness and debauchery. I gained quite a reputation my first year, you know. Anything I could do to put a black mark on the Hollingsworth name, I was all for it."

"To get back at your father."

"Yes. He didn't approve of my course of study. He thought those who lived in faraway lands were savages. If he had lived, he would have forbidden my expeditions. He died during my first year at Oxford. So he never heard about my debauches. Or if he did, he didn't care enough to do anything about it."

It didn't feel right to say I was sorry when he clearly wasn't, so I chose to pursue the subject that most interested me. "When did you meet Ellen?"

"Salverton arranged for a holiday celebration at the end of Michaelmas term of our second year. At his home. Both ladies and gentlemen were invited to attend. Robert brought her along as his guest. They were engaged by then. She was lovely, soft-spoken. Clearly, she adored Robert as her gaze rarely wavered from him."

His tone had taken an intimate tone as he glanced out the window seemingly leaving me, and the train compartment behind, so lost in his own world was he.

"I was instantly smitten. Indeed, most of the other gentlemen seemed to be as well. There was something ethereal, other worldly about Ellen."

"You fell in love with her."

His gaze returned to me. "I did. But Robert had won the prize before I even knew there was one to be won."

"What did you do?"

"I'm no masochist, so I distanced myself from him. I didn't wish to see the glow of happiness on his face. That summer I arrived home to discover Mother had grown quite ill. The physician did not expect her to recuperate. She expressed her wish that Mellie be sent away to the French convent where she'd been educated. She knew of my aspirations to go exploring, and she didn't wish Mellie to be abandoned, much as my father had abandoned her. I did as she wished, of course. I took my six-year-old sister to a place far away from everything she had ever known. She cried the entire trip. Her heart was broken and mine along with her. By the time I began my third year, I was a changed man. Applying myself to my studies, I managed to obtain my degree. By the time I graduated, Robert's engagement was off. I couldn't summon so much as a smidgen of sympathy. Mother had died that year, and I was in too much pain."

"I'm so sorry. You must have cared for her deeply."

"I did. She was the one bright, shining star in my life. Losing her was like losing a part of me."

"But now you have your sister."

"Not for long. If things play out the way she hopes, she'll wed the Duke of Andover."

"But you won't be alone. You'll have Robert and me, Salverton, your friends." I leaned forward. "Don't tell Robert, but I do believe Mother prefers you to him."

He laughed at my attempt at levity. "Oh, somehow I don't think so, but thank you for that. I apologize for turning so maudlin."

"We all have our moments, Lord Hollingsworth." God knew I did. But it was time to get the conversation back on track. "Robert never talked to you about what caused the rift between him and Ellen?"

"Not then. But then I ran into him in London where I was busy outfitting a ship for my first expedition. It was to be a short sojourn to South America, one that would last a bare three months. He'd rejoined the police force with the hope of becoming a detective inspector. A week before I was set to sail, I ran into him on the street. He was patrolling Westminster. We made plans for supper that same night. I think we were both eager to mend the rift between us."

"And did you in fact do so?"

"I believe we did. We talked late into the night about everything that had happened. He only mentioned the engagement had ended. He never explained why, nor did I ask."

I was disappointed to say the least. I'd hoped to get more information from him.

"I was glad we had a chance to talk, for life flung us apart once more. Even as I was sailing to South America on my first expedition, Archduke Franz Ferdinand was being murdered by a Serbian which, of course, forced Austria-Hungary to declare war on that country. Others soon became involved. Russia, being an ally of Serbia, mobilized its troops against Austria-Hungary. Germany declared war on Russia and, subsequently, France due to its alliance with Russia. Nor did Germany stop there. Soon it was invading Belgium. Once Germany took that step, Great Britain declared war against Germany. By that time, we'd reached South America. When we learned what had happened, we set sail for home. Most of us enlisted as soon as we landed on the English shore."

"When did you hear from Robert again?"

"Not until the Great War ended. Somehow, I managed to get through unscathed. I returned home after Armistice Day where I found a note from him. He'd been injured and sent home. After he recuperated, Lord Rutledge and his father convinced him to remain in London rather than return to the front. That was his second injury. I doubted he would have survived a third."

I swallowed hard. I could have lost Robert without ever knowing him. "Yes."

"Lord Rutledge worked his contacts and obtained a detective position for Robert with Scotland Yard. But Robert rose through the ranks on his own merit."

"Yes, I know."

"We resumed our friendship after the war and remained so since then."

"I'm so glad he has you in his life. A stout friend is worth all the gold in the world."

The conductor suddenly materialized at our door. "We'll be arriving in Plymouth in fifteen minutes. Please gather your belongings."

"Thank you. We will." I'd learned little about Ellen from him, but so much more about the man he was. It went a long way to explaining why he was so passionate about helping Robert. They'd been, and still were, the best of mates.

CHAPTER 18

REVEREND CLARKSON

I'd arranged a supper at the hotel where we would be staying for our meeting with Reverend Clarkson. Not in the public restaurant, but a private room as the discussion would involve delicate matters. The train thankfully arrived on time which provided sufficient time to bathe and change before we met with Ellen's cousin. A few minutes before eight, the front desk rang to let me know he'd arrived. I then telephoned Hollingsworth and together we made our way to the lobby.

After exchanging pleasantries with the pastor, we sat down to a dinner which surprised me by its excellence. Of course, being this close to the sea, the fish course, a turbot de sole, was excellent, but the vegetables Parisienne were a surprise, and so was the meat course, a roast served with potatoes. For dessert, we enjoyed fruits and three different cheeses.

We held off any discussion until after the dessert plates

were cleared. At that point, we removed to the small drawing room that adjoined the dining area which contained a piano for those who wished to entertain. After we asked for coffee service, Hollingsworth excused himself, promising to return in an hour. He wished to blow a cloud, something which could be done in the hotel's smoking room.

"But surely, Miss Worthington, we should not be left alone," Reverend Clarkson objected. He was a stickler for the proprieties.

"Lord Hollingsworth will return soon enough. In the meantime, no one knows."

"Yes, but—"

"It will be fine, Reverend Clarkson." Better get on with the discussion, before he decided to bolt. "Could you tell me about Ellen?"

"She was lovely, of disposition as well as face."

"Did you know her before she came to Plymouth?"

"Yes, of course. Mother and I visited when she was younger. Years later, I attended a conference at Oxford for my church. A gathering of clerics of all faiths. Although I did not stay in their home, her father graciously invited me to supper one day. She'd just finished boarding school and was barely used to the workings of the house. But the meal was very pleasantly prepared and served. She had the makings of a wonderful wife."

"Were your aspirations leaning in that direction?" It would explain his infatuation with his cousin.

"Indeed, no, Miss Worthington. She was far above my touch. Financially, I mean."

How very odd. His father had been a brother to Ellen's father who'd been, by all appearances, well-off. "But Professor Clarkson was wealthy, was he not?"

"He married into it. The Waverley sisters, her mother's maiden name, inherited a great deal of money from their father. He'd invested wisely in some far east endeavors. When he passed, his fortune came to his two daughters, Ellen's mother and her aunt, Imelda. It was that money that paid for the house she lived in, and I dare say the same could be said for Mister Staunton's residence."

"But your branch of the family was not blessed with such good fortune?"

"Oh, we made do, that's for certain. Enough for Mother to enjoy a comfortable life. But we did not have the wealth that Professor Clarkson and Mister Staunton enjoyed. Their wives' dowries were, of course, given to them upon their marriage. Or so I understand."

"Professor Clarkson and Mister Staunton rose in stature during their marriages. Surely some of their success could be attributed to that."

"Largely because of Mister Waverley. Don't get me wrong, Professor Clarkson was quite gifted, but it was his father-in-law's worth that helped him rise in the ranks. You see, professors can't be seen to be poor as church mice. They must entertain their students and faculty members. With his wife's money, Professor Clarkson indeed did all that. So did Mister Staunton for that matter. That's how he obtained his board of trustees' position at his bank."

"How very interesting."

"That's why we were so surprised when Ellen wrote Mother and asked if she could come stay with us. Mother, of course, was pleased, as she'd always loved Ellen. But we did wonder what had prompted her to do such a thing."

"Mister Staunton accompanied her to Plymouth?"

"He did. We enjoyed dinner that night, and the next day he returned to Oxford."

"Did Ellen explain why she'd come to you?" Of course, I learned that from his testimony at the inquest. But I wished to delve further into that topic.

"The next morning after breakfast, she requested a private audience with Mother and me. That's when she revealed she'd been taken advantage of by someone she knew."

"Did she reveal the man's name?"

"No. She never did. Mother and I both asked, but she refused to share that information."

"How long did she remain with you?"

"A month."

"During that time, did she ever receive any correspondence?"

"Several letters. Oh, and one parcel."

"Do you know who from?"

"The letters were from a friend, maybe two. The parcel was from her father's solicitor."

I noted that in my journal. "Do you know what the parcel contained?"

"No. She didn't mention it. I assumed it was something her father wished her to have."

"So when did she return to Oxford?"

"Just before Christmas."

"Do you know why?"

His complexion turned ruddy. "She wanted to confront the fiend who stole her innocence. He'd done great damage to her. She felt she could never marry an honorable man, as she'd been tainted. She wanted to bring him down. She said she had proof."

That hadn't come out in the inquest.

"What kind of proof?"

"She wouldn't say. I assured her she was indeed worthy and proposed marriage to her. But she smiled that sweet smile of hers and said she wouldn't desire my sacrifice. I assured her it wouldn't be so. I truly loved her. But she shook her head and said it couldn't be so." He removed his glasses and polished them before placing them back on his nose, giving him time to compose himself. "I would have treasured her, Miss Worthington, the rest of my life."

"Yes. I believe you would have." I paused for a moment while he regained his bearings. "You testified at the inquest you didn't escort her back to Oxford."

"I couldn't. Mother had taken a turn for the worse. Her heart. She'd been ailing for some time. The maid of a friend of Mother's was traveling north to visit her family for the holiday, so I arranged for her to accompany Ellen."

"Her name was Mary Perlmutter."

"That's right. I inquired about her since I thought you'd like to know her whereabouts. Several years ago after her mistress died, she obtained a position in London through a domestic agency. That's all I could learn."

"Thank you. That is very helpful." I would ask Lady Emma to find out which one so she could track down Miss Perlmutter.

Hollingsworth returned smelling of cigars and whisky. He took the space on the sofa across from us.

When he reached for some coffee, I said, "It's probably gone cold. You should ring for another pot."

"Not the first time I've drunk it that way." And then proceeded to serve himself a cup.

I turned back to Reverend Clarkson. "Did you see Ellen again?"

"No." His eyes misted with tears. "But then I didn't expect to. After she confronted her seducer, she intended to start a new life somewhere she was not known. She didn't say where."

"How could she afford to do that?"

"She had her dowry. Or what was left of it, anyway."

"What do you mean what was left of it?"

"The day her father died, she discovered most of it was

gone. That's what caused her father's fatal heart attack. They argued about it."

"That didn't come out at the inquest."

"It didn't have anything to do with her murder. She and her uncle didn't wish to ruin her father's reputation, so they'd hushed it up. He wasn't likely to bring it up in such a public setting."

"But how did it disappear?"

"Her father wouldn't say. She only knew it was mostly gone. Before she came to Plymouth, she asked her uncle for what was left. The account was at his bank, you see."

"How much?"

"Five thousand pounds. She brought some with her. She left the rest behind in Oxford."

"Where? Do you know?"

"No. I don't. I didn't ask, and she didn't say. Mister Staunton would more than likely know what happened to her dowry. He'd be the one to ask."

I wouldn't be asking the uncle. Somebody else would handle that enquiry. "At the inquest Mister Staunton testified that he'd received a letter from Ellen stating that she'd married an Australian sea captain and had gone off with him. He said he'd telephoned your home to enquire about it, and your mother verified the information."

"Mother couldn't have done it, Miss Worthington. She was already bedridden. The only thing I can think of is that Ellen herself intercepted the telephone call. She probably expected it and would have asked one of our maids to fetch her if he did."

Well, that certainly explained it. But was it the truth? As I tucked away my notebook in my handbag, Reverend Clarkson had cause to remark. "You remind me of Ellen, you know. There's a strong resemblance. And she wrote in her journal as well."

"She kept a diary?" Her brother had mentioned it. But it was good to have it confirmed.

"Oh, yes. She had it with her when she came to Plymouth. Wrote in it all the time."

"Did she take it with her when she left?"

"Yes. I saw her tuck it away in her handbag, much as you just did."

With his confirmation, it became even more imperative to discover where that diary had gone. The more facts I discovered, the more I realized the diary was the key to the investigation.

CHAPTER 19

A COMMITTEE MEETING

"Would you object if we stop in London for one night?" I asked Hollingsworth the next day on the way to the train station. "I'd like to ask Ned to make enquiries about Ellen's dowry and ask Lady Emma to find Mary Perlmutter."

"Of course, I don't mind. I'd like to see Melly and hear how the preparations for her debut are progressing."

"Thank you for your kindness and patience, Lord Hollingsworth."

"It's the least I can do."

"I'll send a telegram at the station to let Ned and Mother know we're coming."

"That would be best."

We took care of the message before boarding the London-bound train. As we had five hours of travel, I took advantage of the time to read over my notes and organize them into some kind of order. While doing so, it occurred to me I should get Hollingsworth's opinion on a certain matter.

"You've been at the inquest. I've shared with you everything Mrs. Swanson and Oliver Clarkson as well as the Reverend's statements you missed. You knew Ellen, even if only for a short while."

"Yes."

"What do you think was her state of mind while at Plymouth?"

"A man stole her virtue. She must've been devastated."

"He had to have been someone known to her, don't you think?"

"I do. She led quite a sheltered life. So it stands to reason the man was a friend of the family or a student of her father's." There was a pause. "Unfortunately, Robert qualifies as both."

I huffed out my answer. "We know it wasn't him."

"It's hard to prove a negative, Kitty. You must prepare yourself for the possibility he might be charged with the murder." His eyes communicated nothing but kindness.

He was right, of course, but I refused to entertain the notion. "Not if we find the killer first."

We spent the rest of the trip in silence. He read the newspaper, while I continued making notes. We only engaged in desultory conversation when there was a call for it. Frankly, after two days of traveling and conducting a murder investigation, we both needed some time alone with our thoughts.

After reaching London in the early afternoon, we headed straight to Worthington Manor where Mother welcomed us with open arms. Hollingsworth remained only long enough to reacquaint himself with his sister. As he had a private matter to attend to, he soon excused himself, but not before promising to return for supper. I proceeded to my room where after a bath I laid down to rest. What seemed like only minutes later, Grace woke me so I could dress for dinner.

I wished nothing more than to talk to Robert about what I'd learned, but since he'd forbidden any communication between us, I couldn't do so. But that didn't mean I would cease my enquiries. Except for Margaret and Sebastian, every member of the investigative committee was present and eager to become involved in the investigation, including Lady Aurelia who refused to be left out. So, after supper, we adjourned to the library to discuss the case.

Of course, the first order of business was to bring everyone up to speed. Everyone was so enthralled by the narrative Hollingsworth and I presented no one interrupted us while we talked. Not even Marlowe.

"As you can see," I said, "we have plenty of questions, and few answers. I know how busy all of you are. Ned with Worthington & Son, Ladies Lily and Melissande with the preparations for your debut, Ladies Emma and Aurelia with agency matters. And Lord Marlowe with—You have me. I don't know what keeps your days occupied, but I'm sure there must be something."

He arched a brow. "My estate, Kitty. I'm not the fribble you think I am."

"I think no such thing, Lord Marlowe. I apologize if you misunderstood my meaning."

He flashed that charming smile of his. "No harm done."

Before proceeding, I took a deep breath. Hopefully, I wouldn't ruffle any more feathers. "The way I see it the investigation should be conducted in several fronts. The easiest is to find out what happened to Ellen's dowry. Ned, you're the logical one to manage that enquiry."

"I wouldn't call it easy, Kitty. Those events happened a decade ago. Heaven knows if any records still exist. But I will do my best."

"Thank you, Ned." So much for my hope of avoiding feather ruffling.

"Forgive me for interrupting," Lady Aurelia said, "but wouldn't the uncle be a logical person to ask? After all, the money was in deposit at his bank."

"Yes, of course. But before we approach him, I'd like to have as much information as possible about the dowry. Another matter that needs to be clarified is Professor Clarkson's estate. Her brother, Oliver, inherited it. But he was a minor at the time, so there had to be a guardian. We need to know that person's name."

"I can do that." Ned made a note in the small journal he'd retrieved from his coat.

Lady Emma raised her hand.

"Yes?"

"I've been mulling something over."

I motioned her to continue.

"Ellen Clarkson fled to Plymouth because she wanted to escape an impossible situation. Her father's death; the loss of her dowry."

As well as the loss of her virtue. But I did not wish to mention that at this time. The subject would keep to a later time. "Yes."

"We don't have proof of any of that."

"What do you mean?"

"Reverend Clarkson revealed at the inquest that Ellen's innocence had been stolen. He told you about the loss of her dowry. The argument she had with her father. What if none of that was true?"

"You think he lied?" Lady Melissande interjected. "He's a man of God."

"And men of God never lie?" Lady Emma countered. "It will all need to be confirmed by a second source."

"Yes, of course. Ned will handle the dowry matter, so

we'll find out one way or the other. As far as her loss of innocence, that will be trickier." So much for trying to avoid that subject.

"She must have had a maid, Kitty," Lady Lily volunteered. "She would know. I can't imagine such a thing happening without her maid knowing about it."

"We'll be locating the maid, of course. Her uncle should know where she's gone. We'll ask him when we talk to him. Thank you for bringing it up."

"May I ask a question?" Lady Melissande asked.

"Of course."

"Let's say she was violated."

A murmur ran though the room which I ignored.

"Why would she tell her aunt and cousin?"

"She was seeking refuge at their home."

"But she didn't have to mention it. They would have gladly taken her in. They did take her in. She could have simply said she was seeking peace after the death of her father. She needn't have mentioned it."

"I hadn't thought of that, but you're right. So the question becomes why would she have done such a thing?"

"Because of what she was planning to do," Lady Aurelia said in a calm voice.

"Please explain."

"She wanted to confront her abuser and make him pay for what he'd done to her."

"What good would that do her?" Lady Lily asked.

"Satisfaction. She could then have gotten on with her life," I said.

"But she could have gotten on with her life without confronting him. She had what was left of her dowry. Five thousand pounds would be more than enough for her to live on. If she intended to disappear, she could have taken the train and done so. No. There was more to it than that."

"Something happened after she arrived in Plymouth," Marlowe said. "Didn't you say she received some letters and a parcel from her father's solicitor?"

"She did."

"Something in them must have forced her to return to Oxford," Lady Emma said.

"But what?" Lady Aurelia asked.

"I don't know," I said. "We need more information." I brushed a hand across my brow. I'd hoped for at least some clarity. Instead, we had more questions.

"May I say something?" Hollingsworth asked.

"Of course."

"She was kind, Kitty. She wasn't the revengeful type."

"What happened changed her, Hollingsworth, as it would any woman. She wanted her pound of flesh," I said. "Reverend Clarkson said she had proof."

"It had to be in her diary," Lady Aurelia said. "Reverend Clarkson said she kept one."

"But would she have written an account of that man's perfidy in it? Or been too ashamed to do so? What would happen if it fell into the wrong hands?"

"The police might have confiscated it when they searched the house."

"No. That could not have happened. She took the diary with her to Plymouth. As far as we know, she never returned to her home in Oxford."

"But what if she did, Kitty? It would be the perfect place for her to lie low. The house was shuttered. Nobody was there."

I sighed. "There's no help for it. I'll need to return and thoroughly search the house."

"You'll need her brother's approval."

Easier said than done.

CHAPTER 20

RETURN TO OXFORD

The next day Hollingsworth had a matter to attend to that would take up most of the morning, so we would not be returning to Oxford until the early afternoon. Taking advantage of the time available to me, I accompanied Lady Emma to the agency. I not only wished to become familiar with any matters that had come up but assure myself my absence had not placed an undue workload on her and Lady Aurelia. Although if the latter were true, I had no idea what I could do about it.

As it turned out, the opposite was true.

"Do you mean to tell me business has dried up?" I asked. "How could that be?"

"It's the papers, Miss," Betsy piped up. I'd invited her to join our discussion since she was as much a part of the agency as we were.

Lady Emma found issue with Betsy's comment. "Betsy, maybe we better not—"

"No. I want to know," I interrupted. "What about the papers?" Betsy kept copies of the popular London newspapers, mainly so we could refer to them if there was need.

She handed me several issues of *The Tell-All*, as well as other gossip rags. The headlines were explanation enough. *In Love with a Murderer*, one read. The article detailed my courtship with Robert, ending with the latest accusations against him. *Lady Detective Flouts the Law*. That one alleged I'd somehow gotten Robert to break the law on behalf of my clients. The last one was the most lurid of all. Its headline screamed *Detective's Love Child*.

Unable to read further, I slapped the newspaper against the desk. "Oh, for heaven's sake. When exactly did I have this love child?"

"It's not yours it's screaming about, Miss. It's Detective Crawford's."

"Of all the— How dare they? What love child?"

"It claims he got Ellen Clarkson with child. She fled to Plymouth in shame so she could have their babe in secret."

"There isn't a scintilla of proof of such a thing."

"It doesn't stop them from printing such lies, Kitty," Lady Emma said.

"So our business has suffered because of these monstrous falsehoods?" I asked.

"That's what we're guessing. We still have the looky-loos, and the press, of course. But clients have pretty much stopped coming."

Just then there was a knock on the door.

Betsy walked over to see who it was.

"Is Miss Worthington here?" A masculine voice asked.

"No, she's not."

"Who is it, Betsy?"

"A reporter, Miss. He's been here before."

"Have him come in."

"No, Kitty," Lady Emma urged, panic in her voice.

"Don't, Miss Worthington," Lady Aurelia seconded. "No good can come of this."

I crossed my arms across my chest. "They want a quote. I'll give it to them."

The reporter took a seat on the settee across from the three of us. Betsy stood sentinel to our right.

"Adam Ridgwell, reporter for *The Tell All*."

"Was that your piece in yesterday's paper?" I asked. "The one about the love child?"

"No, ma'am. Donovan Croft wrote that."

"You may tell Mister Croft—"

"Kitty," Lady Emma cautioned.

"That article is a pack of lies," I spit out.

"May I quote you on that?"

"Yes. Robert Crawford is an honorable man. He did not seduce Miss Clarkson, nor did he murder her."

"All evidence to the contrary."

"There is no evidence against him."

"He was engaged to her. He broke off the engagement."

"He did not. It was mutually agreed upon. He testified to that at the inquest."

"And you believe him?"

"Of course, I do."

"There was a witness, Miss Worthington. A maid who overheard their conversation. It was Mister Crawford who ended the engagement."

I asked Mister Ridgwell to leave after that.

"He's lying. That's what they do," Lady Emma said. "He just wanted a reaction from you."

"Well, he got it." I had thrown him out. Needing a moment to settle my nerves, I strode into my office.

"Would you like a cuppa, Miss?" Betsy asked. Sweet thing that she was, she'd noticed my distress.

"Thank you, Betsy, but no. I must return home. I promised Mother I'd join her for lunch." I pressed her hands. "I do appreciate the offer." But there was one more thing I needed to ask before I went on my way. "Lady Emma, I need you to look into something."

"Of course. Anything you need."

"A maid accompanied Ellen back to Oxford. Her name is Mary Perlmutter. At some point in the last ten years, she left her employ at Plymouth and obtained a position in London through a domestic agency. We need to find out where she is so we can talk to her."

"Consider it done."

"I'll help," Lady Aurelia offered.

"Thank you, both. I know you will come through with what I need. Now, I better leave. Hollingsworth is picking me up in an hour." I couldn't help the dejected tone to my voice.

"Kitty, it will be all right. You'll see," Lady Emma said. "If you need anything else, please let us know. We will be more than glad to help."

"I will." My thoughts were too much in turmoil to say more than, "Thank you."

Hollingsworth was already at Worthington Manor which Mother appreciated, although she'd had to postpone the luncheon until my arrival. As I wasn't much of a conversationalist during the meal, Ladies Lily and Melissande filled the void with chatter about their debut season. All the while, Mother gazed at me out of worried eyes.

Afterward, everyone gathered at the foyer to see us off.

It wasn't until we were on the train to Oxford that Hollingsworth asked, "What happened to get you so upset?"

"A reporter came to the agency. He said there's a witness who overheard the conversation between Robert and Miss Clarkson. According to her, it was Robert who ended the engagement. It was not mutually agreed upon."

"Either the witness is lying, or the reporter is. He wanted to get a reaction from you."

"Well, he got it. I threw him out."

Amusement etched his features.

"It's not funny!"

"I apologize." His laughter stopped. "Well, now you know not to talk to them. They'll do anything to sell papers."

"You're right. I should have known better. Ladies Emma and Aurelia tried to stop me, but I wouldn't listen."

"What are you planning to do next?"

"Talk to Letitia Fairbright."

"Ellen's friend?"

"Yes. Her only friend from what Mrs. Swanson told me. Ellen would have confided in her."

"What about her uncle? Somebody will need to talk to him."

"We'll have to wait for Ned's report. He might lie if he has something to hide. No sense talking to him without knowing the facts. Many of the individuals closest to Miss Clarkson may very well have secrets they don't wish to be known. It will be difficult to discover them." My shoulders slumped.

"What's wrong?"

"Last night I realized I'm not being objective."

"Your love for Robert is clouding your judgment."

"Which is why I'll need to depend on others more than usual to set me on the right path. You will tell me if I stray, Lord Hollingsworth?"

"You can be assured of that, Kitty. You can count on Lord Salverton as well. He's grown quite interested in the matter."

"Has he? Why? He's barely familiar with Robert."

"It offends his sense of justice. He will be a powerful ally. Not only because of his status, but his familiarity with Oxford."

"I will be immensely grateful for his assistance, and yours. Heaven knows I need all the help I can get to solve this case."

Since Oxford was only an hour's travel from London, we soon arrived at its station. In no time at all, we were at Margaret's home.

Her very proper butler greeted us with his usual dignity. "Their Graces are expecting you in the study."

"Thank you, Maxwell. I know the way. Can you arrange for someone to take my bag upstairs?"

"Of course, Miss Worthington."

Hollingsworth and I arrived at Margaret's study to find her and Sebastian on the sofa holding hands. The solemn expressions on their faces should have clued me in to the state of things, but it didn't.

"Dear Kitty," Margaret said.

The look she sent me, set off an alarm within me. "What's wrong?"

"Robert's been arrested."

CHAPTER 21

AN ARREST IS MADE

An image of Robert's body swinging from the gibbet materialized unbidden and unwanted in my head. By sheer force of will, I did not collapse. But I must have looked as if I would because Hollingsworth took hold of my elbow and helped me to the sofa.

Sebastian rose to pour brandy into a snifter and handed it to me. "Here."

I drank it in one gulp which, of course, set off a coughing fit. It took me a moment to regain my breath. "Who? When? How?" Heavens! I sounded like an idiot.

"This morning," Margaret said, capturing my hands, rubbing them to infuse some warmth. "Chief Detective Inspector Gordon from the Oxford constabulary arrested Robert at his hotel. Apparently, after interrogating him he'd told Robert not to leave town."

"How did you find out?"

"Robert telephoned to let us know. There's also an article

in the afternoon edition of *The Oxford Crier.*" She pointed to the newspaper that rested on the table in front of her.

"What does the article say?" I wasn't yet strong enough to read it.

"It reported the arrest."

"Of course, it did." Those vultures never missed a chance for a scoop.

"And then it rehashed the inquest. Another piece paid tribute to Professor Clarkson and how much he meant to the Oxford community."

"In other words, they're making a saint of the man while pillorying Robert. Anything else?"

"A shorter article about Ellen. Someone interviewed her pastor. Apparently, she spearheaded the Gift Baskets for the Poor Holiday Program."

"I thought she didn't socialize."

"She would be allowed to go to church, Kitty."

"Yes, of course." I picked up the paper. Gave it a cursory review. "These articles are poisoning the jury pool. If that keeps up, Robert won't stand a chance." My breath hitched.

Hollingsworth dropped to his knees in front of me. "How can I help?"

"I'll write a letter to Robert. If you could come by tomorrow and deliver it to him, I would be most appreciative."

"Yes, of course." He didn't voice the obvious. Robert had prohibited me from contacting him.

Hollingsworth came to his feet. "I better go. I must alert Salverton about this latest development. He has contacts with members of the Oxford community. Maybe he'll have some ideas as to what can be done."

I raised a tear-streaked face to him. "Thank you."

"No need to thank me, Kitty." He addressed Sebastian. "Since Robert had been arrested, he'll need a barrister.

"He has one. He told me so last time I talked to him."

"There's been a change," Margaret said. "He's coming up from London in the morning train."

"Who?" I asked.

"Sir Frederick Stone," Sebastian answered. "He's one of the finest barristers in England."

"Isn't he defending the peer involved in that trust scandal?" Hollingsworth asked.

"Margaret's father arranged it," Sebastian answered. "That's all I know."

"Father knows about this?"

"We telephoned him as soon as we heard from Robert," Margaret said. "A couple of hours later, he called back with Sir Frederick Stone's name."

With Father's connections, he'd probably moved mountains to get Sir Frederick to represent Robert.

Hollingsworth glanced at his watch. "Now, I really must go. I'll call tomorrow morning at nine for the letter."

"I'll have it ready for you," I said.

Once he was gone, Margaret came to her feet, bringing me up with her. "Dearest, it's been a rather long day for you. Why don't you go lie down in your room and get some rest? I'll have my maid bring you a supper tray."

"You don't have to cosset me about, Margaret. I'll come down when it's time for dinner."

"Sebastian and I are attending a fundraising supper event for an Oxford women's health clinic. It was scheduled before . . . all this happened. I can't cry off as I'm one of the sponsors. I hope you understand."

"Yes, of course. I don't expect you to put your life on hold for me."

"We're not, I promise. You will be fine?" Concern poured from her every pore. She was clearly worried about me.

I put on my brightest smile. "Of course. I'll have plenty to occupy my time as I must write that letter to Robert."

"Very well." She squeezed my hand. "We'll talk tomorrow."

"Absolutely."

I made my way up the stairs to my chamber where Margaret's maid, Sarah, waited for me. After she made me as comfortable as she could, she drew the shades and left me to my solitude. But my troubled thoughts would not allow me to rest.

Supper was a gay affair. Brought to me on a tray with a rose in a silver bud vase, it consisted of chicken cordon bleu, potatoes Parisienne, and asparagus in a hollandaise sauce. For dessert, I was treated to a floating island with lemon-scented custard sauce and raspberries. A pinot Grigio accompanied the meal. Having had little to eat for the last couple of days, I rediscovered my appetite and did justice to it. Sarah had very kindly brought coffee for after the meal. I was glad of it. It helped me stay awake as I struggled to put words to paper.

Hours later, after many attempts, I'd managed to write a two-page letter that outlined what we'd discovered and what I was hoping to do. It was not scintillating prose, but it would do. I ended the letter with 'All my love, Your Catherine.'

It was three in the morning before I lay down to sleep. I'd asked Sarah to wake me at eight. I was not exactly chipper when she did. But Hollingsworth was expected within the hour, so I forced myself to rise. Bathed and dressed, I descended the stairs just in time to see him shown in by Maxwell.

He brought news of his own, so even though he'd already enjoyed breakfast, he joined me in the dining room. "Salverton has gathered information of note."

"Such as?"

"About fifteen years ago, whispers abounded about the Northern Savings and Trust."

"The uncle's bank?"

"Yes."

"Apparently, some funds had been 'mislaid.'

"Is that another word for stolen?"

"No one knew. It was apparently very hush-hush. People were making noises about going to the police, but Mister Staunton promised everything would be all right. And then, lo and behold, the funds were 'found.'"

"Really?"

"The amount that had gone missing amounted to 25,000 pounds."

"How did he account for it?"

"Bookkeeping error. The funds never left the bank; they'd just been allocated to the wrong account. Or so he said. He promised a full audit of the error, which was carried out. The unrest died down. But—"

"Yes?"

"There were some who were unsatisfied with the explanation. They urged stronger oversight protection over the bank. That's when additional seats were assigned to the Board of Trustees."

"I'll alert Ned since he's the one looking into the financial matters. Anything else?"

He laughed. "It's only been twelve hours, Kitty. Give us time."

"Robert may not have time," I said in all seriousness.

He sobered up in a hurry. "Yes, of course."

As we were making our way from the dining room, Margaret and Sebastian appeared, arms around each other's waists.

"Good morning," I said.

"Morning," Margaret whispered.

"How did it go?"

Margaret stifled a yawn. "We raised 2,000 pounds. The money will be put to good use. We have our eye on property close to the center of town, and I'm close to choosing an administrator for the clinic."

"I don't know how you manage with your studies and a brand-new husband."

"I'm not complaining," Sebastian said, before pointing to the food on the sideboard. "We better eat before the food goes cold."

"Yes, of course. Talk to you soon, Kitty. Lord Hollingsworth."

As we made our way to the front door, Hollingsworth reminded me about his errand, not that I was likely to forget. "Do you have the letter?"

"Yes." I opened the leather portfolio I'd brought with me and handed him the envelope addressed to Robert. "Please make sure he reads it."

"I'll do my best."

With that I had to be satisfied.

CHAPTER 22

SIR FREDERICK STONE

But it wasn't Hollingsworth who showed up later that afternoon. I was in my room going over my notes when Sarah knocked on my door. "Begging your pardon, Miss, but there's a gentleman downstairs who wishes to speak with you."

Hollingsworth! I took the stairs two at a time, eager to see what he had to say. But it wasn't the marquis who awaited me in the drawing room. But an older gentleman, dressed all in black, in his fifties, dark, silver-streaked hair, and piercing blue eyes.

"Miss Worthington?"

"Yes, I'm afraid you have the better of me."

"Sir Frederick Stone."

"Robert's barrister?"

"Yes. I came to return your letter." He handed it to me, unopened.

He must have seen the ire in my eyes because his brow arched in response. "I can see you're upset."

"Yes, I am. You have no right to do this."

"Miss Worthington. May I sit?"

"Yes, of course. Where are my manners? Would you like some tea? Or coffee?"

"No. I can't stay long. I'm on the next train back to London, which leaves"—He glanced as his pocket watch—"in half an hour."

"You should have gone to the station, sir, so as not to miss it. The letter could have been mailed back to me."

"I deemed this visit more important."

I folded my arms in front of me to keep them from trembling. "How so?"

"Miss Worthington, you are not to contact your fiancé."

I firmed up my chin. "Why not, sir?"

"Because you can put his defense, indeed his very life, in jeopardy. You are not married. You're not his legal counsel. Your communications with him are not privileged. The police can demand you share with them anything he says."

"He has not shared anything that puts him in jeopardy."

"I understand you've already visited him twice. You can't possibly determine what the law will make of your conversations with him."

"We were careful. He didn't say anything—"

"Miss Worthington." He was practically yelling, so angry was he. "Do you want Inspector Crawford to swing from a gibbet?"

My worst nightmare. "No," I said in a small voice. "Of course not."

"Then I beg you not to contact him. I've told him under no circumstances is he to see you, talk to you, communicate with you. You must obey that edict. Is that clear?"

Margaret arrived somewhat breathless. "Is something the matter? I heard loud voices."

"Margaret, this is Sir Frederick Stone, Robert's barrister. Sir Frederick, this is my sister, the Duchess of Wynchcombe."

"How do you do, ma'am?"

"Your Grace. She is to be addressed as Your Grace."

"Oh, Kitty, please. Let us not stand on formalities. An honor to meet you, Sir Frederick. What's the word on Robert?"

"As you can appreciate, Your Grace," he said, pointedly glancing at me, "I'm unable to share that information as it must remain confidential."

"Yes, of course."

"Mister Crawford informed me you're conducting an investigation into Ellen Clarkson's murder."

I hitched up my chin. "I am. You don't intend to forbid that as well?"

"On the contrary. I encourage you to do so. I would be interested in knowing what you discover."

"I will keep you apprised, sir."

He gazed at me with his piercing blue eyes as if he was trying to divine my thoughts. He must have approved of what he saw because he nodded. "Good. Now, I really must go if I'm to catch that train." But before he left, he took Margaret aside. "She is not to communicate with my client."

"May I think of him, Sir Frederick?" I asked in a peevish tone.

"As long as you don't share your thoughts with him, think away." And with that last pithy statement, he marched out. Margaret accompanied him to the foyer to say a polite good-bye, but she was soon back in the drawing room.

Glaring out the window, I emphatically stated. "Impossible man."

"Kitty, the way you addressed him was extremely rude. You know better than to behave in such a manner."

Appropriately admonished, I turned to her, my cheeks no doubt blazing with heat. "You're right. I was. I'll write him a note of apology. I'm just so angry, frustrated—"

"Wanting to bash your head against the wall?"

"Yes," I let out a watery laugh. "I'm so sorry, Margaret. I'm acting like an idiot."

"Dearest." She embraced me. "I understand. I felt the same way when Sebastian was in jail."

"But that was different."

"How?"

"I don't know. It just was."

She shook with laughter. "You're making no sense, you know."

I dropped into the settee. "It's horrible not knowing how he's doing. If I could only talk to him. Five minutes would do."

"No, it wouldn't. You'd want to do it all over again the next day and the next. Trust me. I know."

"I'm being such an imposition. Here you are, a newly married woman, with your studies, and your causes. And I'm totally interfering with your life."

"First of all, you're not stopping me from doing anything I wish to do. I attended that fundraiser last night, didn't I? And second"—it was her turn to have rosy cheeks—"Sebastian and I very much enjoy our private moments."

"I'm glad of that."

"And even if it were different, Kitty, I wouldn't be married to the man I love if it weren't for you. With all the evidence against him, you discovered the true culprit. Do you honestly think there is anything I wouldn't do for you?"

"I didn't do it alone, you know. Everyone helped."

"True. But you were the one who figured it out." She

paused for a moment. "Come to think of it, that's what's wrong."

"What do you mean?"

"You're missing your committee."

"We discussed matters in London."

"But everything's here. In Oxford. You need to have a sit-down like you usually do. We'll do that tonight. You and me and Sebastian. I'll telephone Hollingsworth and Salverton. They'll want to be included. We'll do it after supper tonight."

"Invite Lady Delphine as well."

She wrinkled her nose. "Are you sure? Hollingsworth and Salverton will be here."

"She's very bright, and she has no desire to marry. That's her mother's idea. She wants to be a modiste and open her own shop."

"Really?"

"Yes. I told her you'd share your tried-and-true methods for avoiding a proposal."

Margaret laughed. "You didn't?"

"I did. You see, dear sister, you were so very good at it."

"I was, wasn't I?" She broke into laughter, and I joined her.

Sebastian chose that moment to walk in. "What's so amusing?"

Margaret flew up, straight into his arms. "We're having a dinner party tonight and afterwards we're holding a meeting of the Investigative Committee. Won't that be fun?"

All Sebastian could do was smile and kiss her.

CHAPTER 23

THE OXFORD INVESTIGATIVE COMMITTEE

That afternoon while Margaret made the arrangements and telephoned our invitees, I withdrew to my room to review my notes. What we'd discovered. What the London Investigative Committee had discussed. What needed to be done. Going through that process settled my mind which meant I could look at things methodically once more. Margaret was right. This was exactly what I needed.

Margaret stopped in to tell me all three of our guests had accepted, although Salverton had done so reluctantly. He'd feared he'd be in for another matchmaking attempt. Once she assured him that was not the case, he said yes. So it was that we sat six for supper and, I must say, had a merry old time. Hollingsworth entertained us with a seafaring adventure while Salverton countered with tales of his elusive stamp hunts. Filled with bonhomie, good cheer, and not a small amount of wine, we gathered afterward in the library to discuss the investigation.

With Margaret assigned as our notetaker, her past task, I explained the process to Salverton and Lady Delphine. They nodded seriously, and not so seriously. You can guess which one did what. Salverton and Lady Delphine had resided here most of their lives, while Hollingsworth, Sebastian, and Margaret had studied at Oxford. So, they all held unique positions in the investigation. They were familiar with Oxford society, university academia, and the everyday persons one normally meets.

Having said all that, I summarized what we'd learned and where we stood ending with, "Any questions?"

"Not about the process," Salverton said. "You've explained it splendidly."

"Thank you, Lord Salverton. Let us proceed then. As I see it, we have at least three avenues of investigation. People, places, and things. As far as the people are concerned, we have the main players, Reverend Clarkson, Mister Staunton, and Professor Burgess. Hollingsworth and I have already talked to the pastor. He pointed us toward the issue of the dowry."

"One of the things," Lady Delphine said.

"Yes, indeed. My brother, Ned, is looking into the dowry from his end, but there's nothing to say we can't investigate it as well."

"Hear, hear," Sebastian said.

"Now, Lord Salverton, you're familiar with Mister Staunton, Ellen's cousin by marriage."

"Yes, I am. He's the chair of the Board of Trustees at the Northern Bank & Trust."

"And some years ago, there was an issue of 'lost funds.' Would you care to explain that to us?"

"Of course." He summarized what Hollingsworth had already explained.

"I remember that," Lady Delphine said. "Father was quite upset as he held some of his funds there. He withdrew them as a result."

"Many people did," Lord Salverton said. "It took some years for the bank to regain the trust of the Oxford community."

"Would you, and Lady Delphine as well, be willing to talk to those who were affected?" Another 'thing' that needed to be examined.

"Yes, of course."

Lady Delphine nodded. "I'd be amenable to talking to people. At least two of Father's acquaintances had grave concerns."

"Splendid. If you could do that as soon as you can. I've telephoned Ned and asked him to look into this matter as well."

"What about talking to Mister Staunton himself?" Lady Delphine asked.

"That conversation needs a woman's touch," I said.

"Would you like me to discuss it with him?" Margaret asked. "I think he will respond to my title."

"You're so busy. I hate to ask."

"Not too busy for this. I've finished my paper. Another one is not due for two weeks. I have time."

"Thank you, Margaret. We'll discuss later what I'd like to know."

"Now, Sebastian, you were part of academia for a while. I'd like you to talk to Professor Burgess. Find out as much information as you can about his life, his relationship with Professor Clarkson, and Ellen. Oh, and young Oliver Clarkson. Try to find out his whereabouts during the days before Christmas 1913. We need to know if he was in town."

"I'll flatter him. Tell him I need to discover something related to whatever he teaches."

"History," Margaret said.

"Perfect. I have the perfect topic. The role of botany in England's growth as an empire."

"How the devil would he know that?" Salverton asked.

"He wouldn't, but he'd know someone who did. And that person would end up pointing me to my own study. It's in the Bodleian Library, don't you know?" He said with a broad grin. "Let's just hope that person doesn't realize Sebastian Dalrymple and the Duke of Wynchcombe are one and the same."

"Well, that's Professor Burgess and Mister Staunton taken care of."

"What about Edwin Clarkson?" Hollingsworth asked. "He deserves a second look."

He was right. We only had Reverend Clarkson's word for certain matters regarding Ellen which meant we would have to learn whether he was an honest man. Unfortunately, it would involve more travel. "I'm afraid it will mean another trip to Plymouth to talk to people who know him."

"Which I will be glad to do. If I leave tomorrow, I can be back in two days."

"Are you sure?"

"Do you need to ask?" he asked with a cheeky grin.

"Very well. You know what we need to discover." Of all the people present, he was the one most familiar with the investigation.

"Now that we've discussed the main players involved, who else do we need to talk to?"

"The woman who accompanied her on the train, Mary Perlmutter," Lady Delphine said.

"Lady Emma is tracking down her details," I explained.

"What about Ellen's maid?" Margaret asked. "She should be somewhere around Oxford I would imagine."

"At the inquest, the medical examiner said she'd helped identify the remains," Hollingsworth reminded me.

"That's right." I'd forgotten about that. "How do we get that information?"

"Robert's barrister probably has it in his records. If he doesn't, he can request it," Hollingsworth said.

"We did not exactly part in the best of terms," I said, somewhat chagrined.

"He said you should continue your investigation, Kitty," Margaret said. "If he objects, tell him that's exactly what you're doing."

"Very well." But he would be my last resort. There had to be another approach. "Once we learn her whereabouts, I'll talk to her. Anything else?"

"What about Ellen's friend?" Margaret asked. "Not Mrs. Swanson, the other one."

"Letitia Fairbright. I already scheduled some time with her. I understand they remained in touch. Maybe she can add something to what we know. Any other thoughts?"

"There was a chap," Hollingsworth said, almost absent-mindedly.

I had to grin. "A chap?"

"Totally smitten with Ellen. He was also a favorite student of Professor Clarkson's. I remember Robert saying what a nuisance he was." He snapped his fingers. "Thomas Holland. That was his name. Same year as Robert."

"Do you know where he's gone?"

"No. But the registrar's office would."

"I'll find out," Sebastian said.

"Good lad," Salverton said.

I glanced down at my notes. "That's all I have. Unless there's anything else?"

"You mentioned places?" Margaret asked referring to her notes. "What places?"

"Ellen's bedroom. I'm eager to find her diary. Hopefully, her brother will allow me to inspect it once more. So, is that all?"

I was met with silence.

"We'll meet again in four days. At two. Refreshments will be served." I'd already cleared the date with Margaret.

As the meeting broke up, I fell into a conversation with Lady Delphine. I was curious about one thing. "How did you get your mother's approval to attend supper unchaperoned?"

"I told Mother Lords Salverton and Hollingsworth would also be in attendance. She couldn't say yes fast enough."

Lord Salverton apparently overheard because he glared at Margaret. "But you said—"

Lady Delphine had no trouble interpreting that look. "Not to worry Lord Salverton. I have no designs on you. My ambition lies elsewhere."

"Oh, ho!" Salverton nudged Hollingsworth who appeared dumbstruck.

"Not Lord Hollingsworth either," Lady Delphine said with a grin.

Hollingsworth breathed an easy sigh. "Some other gentleman, perhaps."

Her lips twitched with amusement. "Why, no gentleman at all."

Now, it was Salverton's turn to go slack-jawed.

Lady Delphine stifled a laugh. "The expression on your face, Lord Salverton. I can't even begin to imagine what you're thinking."

"Why, nothing at all, Lady Delphine," Salverton said. "Isn't that right, Hollingsworth?"

"Speak for yourself, mate. I've seen plenty on my travels.

But I gather Lady Delphine is not speaking about a personal relationship."

"You're right, Lord Hollingsworth. How very clever of you. I want to open my own modiste shop in London. Father has promised to foot the bill as long as I gain Mother's approval. She will only give it if I don't receive any proper marriage proposals this season. Her Grace—"

"Margaret, please."

"Margaret has kindly agreed to give me a few suggestions on how to avoid them. I asked her when she telephoned."

"Indeed, I will."

"Well, in that case, if I can be of help, dear lady, I will be glad to do so." Salverton bowed over Lady Delphine's hand and kissed it.

"Thank you. That is very kind of you, milord."

Margaret and I glanced at each other. We'd seen this dance before. Marlowe, confirmed bachelor that he was, had eschewed matrimony until he became better acquainted with Lady Emma and fallen madly in love.

"What will you do?" Hollingsworth asked, taking me aside.

"Talk to Letitia Fairbright. She was one of Ellen's friends at boarding school. Maybe she can add something to what we know."

"One can only hope."

CHAPTER 24

LETITIA FAIRBRIGHT

Miss Fairbright turned out to be a fount of information. Currently a lecturer at Oxford, her name matched not only her academic qualifications but her coloring as well. She had a fair complexion and hair a violent shade of red. She'd indeed stayed in touch with Ellen. Although their lives had taken different paths, their friendship hadn't wavered.

"We shared sleeping quarters at the Brewster Academy. We were quite different in our approach to academics. I was a very serious student, you see. Ellen simply wished to get through her studies. She missed home awfully, especially her mother, who'd died in childbirth. I believe she was only twenty-six at the time."

"Mrs. Swanson said the same."

"Although we were different in our academic pursuits, at the end of the day we celebrated our triumphs and commiserated about our failures. We forged a bond that stood the test of time."

"You were fortunate. Boarding school can be a rather lonely experience. Or so I've heard."

"You did not attend one?" She seemed surprised.

"No. My mother could not bear to part with her daughters—there were three of us—so she hired the very best teachers she could find. We were all taught at home."

"You received a fine education for the Duchess of Wynchcombe is widely regarded as extremely bright."

"Thank you. She is that." I glanced down at my journal to review my list of questions. "Were you familiar with the time leading to Ellen's engagement to Robert Crawford?"

A soft smile bloomed across her lips. "Yes, indeed, I was. She shared everything with me. Her excitement the day they met, the suppers he attended. The day he proposed. She was giddy with happiness."

"Because she was in love?"

"Yes, of course. But it was more than that. She was thrilled she would have her own household and a family of her own. Something she craved."

This wasn't the first time I heard the same sentiment. Mrs. Swanson had said something similar. It needed to be explored. "Her brother, Oliver Clarkson, allowed me to inspect her room. He'd left it exactly as it had been during her lifetime. I found household accounts, menus. She seemed to work in the capacity of housekeeper. That seemed rather odd to me."

"There was a housekeeper when she was younger. But when Ellen returned from school, she discovered the housekeeper had been dismissed. It was rather chaotic from what Ellen said. So she took on those responsibilities."

"Do you know why the housekeeper was released?"

"Well, it wasn't only the housekeeper but other servants

as well." She hesitated for a moment before she continued. "There seemed to be an issue with the household income. Ellen didn't come right out and say so, mind you. But I got the impression that money was not as abundant as it should have been."

This was the first time I'd heard of this. "But her father was a professor. And when his wife passed away, he would have inherited her estate, which was substantial from what I've heard."

"One would think so. But by the time Ellen finished school, circumstances had changed. During her mother's lifetime, she'd enjoyed many luxuries. A new wardrobe every year, frequent outings to places her mother held dear. And there was a full staff—a housekeeper, a gardener, a cook and her assistant, several maids. But when she returned home, she found the household staff greatly reduced. But it was more than that. Her wardrobe needed to be updated as fashions had changed. But it just wasn't. Season to season, she wore the same clothes."

"Is that why she didn't attend social events? Because she couldn't afford a new wardrobe?"

"Partly that, but also her father feared Oxford society would corrupt her. So, she was only allowed to socialize with those her father invited to suppers at home."

"She must have resented such tight control over her life." I know I would have.

"She did, although she didn't talk about it much. A few comments slipped out now and then, however."

"If she wasn't allowed to socialize, why were you allowed to visit her?"

"I was a serious young woman pursuing my studies at Oxford, so Professor Clarkson gave me his stamp of approval. I was deemed a good influence on Ellen. Of course, we did not wander far from the house. A local tea shoppe, the park across the street. That was as far as we walked. We were always accompanied by her maid."

"Speaking of which, what was her name?"

"Molly Devine. She was the housemaid, but she came along whenever we took a stroll."

"You didn't bring your own?"

"I didn't have one. I had a room at St. Margaret's Hall. Scouts handled all the students' needs. Of course, their duties didn't include escorting young women about. They had enough to do as it was."

"Yes, of course." Curious about her studies, I asked, "What dates did you attend Oxford?"

"From 1912 to 1915."

"So you did not come to Oxford directly after boarding school?"

"No. My family was not well-off. I could not afford the Oxford fees."

"Who paid your expenses at boarding school?" I immediately regretted the question. It had nothing to do with the investigation. "My apologies. I shouldn't have asked."

Her smile communicated kindness. "It's a perfectly reasonable question, Miss Worthington. My family applied for a scholarship so I could attend. I was fortunate to have it awarded. It provided the credentials I needed to attend this university."

"Did you receive the same opportunity at Oxford?"

"Sadly, no scholarships existed for female students. A benefactor paid my fees. Ellen introduced me to him. Professor Burgess." A shadow crossed her face at the mention of the man. "He saw my potential and sponsored me."

"Did you earn a degree?" Not an idle question for Oxford did not begin to award them to women until after Miss Fairbright had finished her studies.

"In 1920 when Oxford deemed women worthy of earning one."

"A pity it took that long. I understand you're now a lecturer at the university."

She brightened up. "Indeed, I am. I hope to make full professor one day."

"A lofty goal. I hope you achieve it someday." I meant it. She would make an excellent professor. "Now, about the maid, Molly Devine. Do you have any idea where she might be?"

"I'm afraid I don't. The uncle kept her on, but when Ellen left for Plymouth, he let her go."

CHAPTER 25

MOLLY DEVINE

Rather than contact Frederick Stone about the maid's whereabouts, I decided to adopt an approach that was suggested by Margaret. "She probably went to a domestic agency after she was dismissed. Hopefully, they have records from ten years back."

After obtaining the information from Maxwell, I telephoned the two domestic agencies in town. Acting as the secretary to the Duchess of Wynchcombe, I said I was looking for a maid, Molly Devine. Her Grace had known her before she assumed the title and was eager to connect with her. "I was wondering if she's in your books. We can offer a very generous salary, as well as a lucrative fee for your agency, of course."

But the lady on the other end of the call did not take the bait. "Let us check, Miss . . . ?" The question hung in the air.

I couldn't provide my real name. "Miss Gladys Trulove," I responded.

"You do realize we don't share this information with just anybody. We will need to verify it."

"Of course. You may call me back." I provided Margaret's telephone number.

Within minutes, the phone rang again. "Miss Trulove. My sincere apologies to have kept you waiting." The agency lady's entire demeanor had changed. "You would not believe the crank calls we receive. University students are always up for a lark."

"I understand. Were you able to locate Miss Devine in your records?"

"Yes, I was. Unfortunately, she's no longer in domestic service."

"Oh, that's disappointing. May I inquire as to the reason why?"

"Her sister became quite ill. She went to live with her at Sandford-on-Thames."

"Would that be Trudy? She was always speaking of her."

"No. Her sister's name is Martha Pruitt. Now, we have several other candidates that I'm sure would meet Her Grace's requirements. Shall I send them over to be interviewed?"

"I'm afraid Her Grace's heart was set on Molly. But I will pass on the information. Thank you for your time."

"Martha Pruitt at Sandford on Thames," I said to myself before turning to Margaret's butler. "Any idea how far from Oxford that is, Maxwell?"

"About five miles, Miss Worthington."

"Very well. Can you telephone Lord Salverton? I'll need his assistance." He had offered to help, and since Hollingsworth was not available, I would have to depend on him.

Salverton assured me he would locate Martha Pruitt's address. "It's a small parish. The vicar will know."

And, of course, the vicar would not hesitate at providing that information to a marquis. Titles worked wonders.

In no time at all, Salverton called back. "You'll be happy to know Martha Pruitt recuperated from her illness. She and her sister live in a cottage in town. Vicar Merryweather will send them a note tonight inquiring whether they can meet with us. He'll telephone me with the time. I suggested eleven. After breakfast and before luncheon. I'll provide a generous donation to the church for his assistance."

"And I'll bring a basket of food for the sisters."

"Jolly good. If there is a problem, I'll ring you back."

"Thank you, Lord Salverton. I appreciate your help."

"You're welcome. This is almost as fun as hunting down one of my stamps."

"You don't really collect those, do you?"

His bonhomie vanished. "Why, whatever do you mean?"

"Ned, my brother, worked for the War Department during the Great War. He recognized your name. He didn't say anything, of course, but it did make me wonder."

"As you say, dear lady, mum's the word."

"Yes, of course."

More than likely, Salverton used stamp collection as a cover to travel to all parts of the world. But if he was one, I'd eat my chapeau.

The following morning, Salverton drove his motorcar, a Rolls Royce Pall Mall Tourer, to Margaret's home. Thankfully, he'd put up the soft top. Still, I was bundled up to the gills in my sister's motoring robe, since I'd failed to bring one of my own, a warm wool cloche and driving gloves. Even though it was a fair, sunny day, it was a bit chilly.

"You'll roast in that thing," Salverton said, squinting at me.

"I like to be toasty warm," I said grabbing the food basket Margaret's cook had kindly prepared.

"Very well." All he wore was a heavy corduroy coat, a cap, and a set of goggles. He handed me a matching set after I settled the basket into the back seat and climbed into the motorcar. "It'll get dusty on the road. You wouldn't want to damage your eyes."

And then, without any warning, he peeled off. Although he kept a sedate pace through the cobblestoned streets of Oxford, once we'd left the city behind, he opened her up. He drove like it was a motorcar race while I hung on for dear life, losing my hat when he swerved to avoid a horse-drawn cart. He didn't lift his foot off the pedal until we made Sandford-on-Thames and screeched to a stop in front of the church.

I shot him a rather scathing look. "Remind me never to get into a motorcar with you again."

"Will do." He jumped from the Rolls to get directions from the vicar which gave my stomach the chance to settle. Thankfully, he drove at a more reasonable speed toward the cottage where Miss Pruitt and Miss Devine lived, probably to give the onlookers a chance to gawk.

The two sisters were expecting us as they opened the door as soon as we knocked. Inside stood two ladies. Their resemblance so strong, one could see how they were related. Both white-haired, with tight curls haloing their heads, and button black eyes. Of slender build, neither had an ounce to spare on her frame. But they were both welcoming as they showed us to the immaculately kept parlor.

"I brought a food basket to show my appreciation," I said.

Taking it from my hands, Miss Devine exclaimed, "Oh, will you take a look, sister? Fresh-baked bread, fruits, cheese, and a jar of honey."

"We thank you, Miss Worthington, but you didn't have to bring a present," Miss Pruitt said.

"It's the least I could do after you agreed to talk to us."

"Oh, it's herself you will be talking to," she said. "I have no knowledge of that household."

"Yes, of course."

"Would you like some elderberry wine? I made it myself."

"That would be lovely, thank you."

She served the wine in dainty crystal glasses along with several biscuits, properly plated of course.

"Those are not tinned. Molly baked them fresh this morning."

"Oh, you shouldn't have."

"'Tis no trouble, Miss," Miss Devine said. "It's not every day a marquis comes calling on us." She batted her lashes at Salverton.

Once again, the title had turned the trick.

"You don't mind if I take notes?" I asked. "It makes it easier to remember what you said."

"No, of course not," Miss Devine said, her adoring gaze still on Salverton.

"How long did you work in the Clarkson household?"

"Twenty years. I was a maid of all work, you see. I cleaned, dusted, kept the place spit spot. Those early days when Mrs. Clarkson was still alive, there were several of us. She had her own ladies' maid, of course. And we had a proper housekeeper."

"That changed?"

"Oh, yes, indeed. After she passed, Professor Clarkson dismissed her maid. Cook's assistant went next. Once he became a widower, he didn't entertain as much. When Miss Ellen finished her schooling, she took on the housekeeper duties, as he began holding gatherings once more. Small ones, at first. Larger ones as Miss Ellen grew older. She became more adept at them, you see. It became harder to keep up with me duties, though, as it was only me to clean."

"Did Miss Ellen have a personal maid?"

"No. I'd do for her whenever she needed help with her clothes and such. She dressed her own hair, though. A lovely dark brown it was. Much like your own, Miss."

"So I've been told." I tried my best to hide my reaction. "What happened the day Professor Clarkson died?"

"I wasn't there when it happened. It was my half day off, so I'd come here to visit me sister. You remember, Martha?"

"Indeed, I do, Sister. You couldn't visit as long as you wished. Cook was suffering from the toothache, and you were going back to help with the supper."

"Indeed, I was. I arrived around half past four. Knew right off something was wrong. No meal was being prepared, you see. Cook sat by the kitchen table, stone-faced. After she told me what happened, I went to Miss Ellen's room. She was lying on that pink bedspread of hers sobbing for all she was worth. Broke my heart it did. I tried to comfort her, but she sent me away."

"Who else was in the house?"

"Professor Burgess, Mister Staunton, and the doctor. They were talking quiet like in Professor Clarkson's study. The body had been taken away."

"What about Oliver, Ellen's brother?"

"Oh, he was in his room. That's where he spent most of his time, among his books and things. He only came out for his meals."

"He hadn't gone out with his friends?"

"He didn't have any. None that I ever saw in any case."

"Was Cook in the house when the professor suffered his heart attack?"

"Oh, indeed, she was, but she'd been having a bit of a lie-down on account of her tooth. She'd taken laudanum for the pain."

"So she didn't witness his death?"

"No, Miss. Not as such. Miss Ellen had to wake her up. She was that fast asleep."

"I see. Have you stayed in contact with Cook?" I'd need to question her as well.

"No, Miss. She got another position after Mister Staunton dismissed her. I heard she fell down some stairs and broke her neck. She was getting on in age, you see."

"I'm sorry."

"She was a merry old soul. Always quick with a laugh."

"I'm sure she'd appreciate you thinking fondly of her."

"Oh, I'll never forget her, Miss."

"So, she was dismissed by Mister Staunton, but you weren't?"

"Miss Ellen insisted I come with her to her aunt and uncle's house. She never got over her father's death, poor mite. She cried and cried." A sudden pause as she wrinkled her brow. "It was odd, though."

"What do you mean?"

"She often seemed more angry than sad."

"Some people act that way," Miss Pruitt said. "It's their way of coping after a loved one dies."

Molly sent her sibling a loving look. "Thank you, Sister, for pointing that out."

"When did you leave that employ?"

Martha huffed, but it was Molly who answered. "I didn't leave, Miss. I was dismissed. When Miss Ellen left for Plymouth, Mister Staunton felt they had no more need for my services. He did provide an excellent reference, so I was able to obtain another position. I stayed there for five years until my dear Martha became ill. So, I came to live with her. As you can see, she happily recovered."

"Thanks to your great nursing." Martha turned to me. "I had the Spanish Influenza, you see."

A sorrow crossed over my heart which must have shown on my face.

"Did you lose someone to that awful disease, dearie?" Martha asked.

"My sister, Emily."

"How very dreadful."

"Yes, it was rather." Mother had been prostrated with grief. So much so, Margaret had assumed the reins of the household, and the handling of all of us. "My sister, Margaret, got us through the worst of it."

"Sisters are such blessings."

"Yes, they are." I glanced down at my notes to give me a chance to regain my composure. "Was Ellen pleased with her engagement to Robert Crawford?"

Miss Devine's face lit up. "Oh, she was the happiest I ever saw her. He was all she talked about. She made so many plans for their future. Wrote about them too in that diary of hers."

"She kept a diary?" Of course, I knew. Still, I wanted her take on things.

"From the time she was little. Kept them all, too."

I hadn't found one in her room, much less several. "Where did she keep them?"

"Beneath her mother's roses, that's what she said. It was rather odd, though."

"Why so?"

"Her mother didn't plant rosebushes. She was partial to lilies and daffodils. When I asked her what she meant, she said it was a secret. And then she laughed in that pleasant way of hers."

I made a note of it, as it was one more clue as to the location of the diaries. "While she was still living at home, did you accompany her when she left the house?"

"Yes, indeed, Miss. Professor Clarkson was very strict about that. When Miss Fairbright visited and they'd go to the park or the tea shoppe, I'd go along. Kept my distance, of course, so they could share their secrets. But I did my duty, I did."

"I'm sure you performed your responsibilities splendidly, Miss Devine. What about after she got engaged?"

"I went along with her and Mister Crawford as well. At least while she was under Professor Clarkson's roof."

"But not when she moved into her aunt and uncle's?"

"It was only the two times. One was when Mister Crawford took her out on a picnic. He was hoping to cheer her up, you see. She told me she didn't require my company as she wanted to be private with him."

"Who was the second person?"

"Professor Burgess. I think he felt a responsibility toward her since he was her father's friend. He'd come by after the funeral, but this was, let me think, must have been October. Anyhow, he came by to visit, and she insisted he take her out for a ride. He had his motorcar with him, you see. She'd been cooped up for some time and needed some air. That's what she said to me. When I offered to go along, she said there was no need. It was only Professor Burgess, after all. And off they went. They didn't come back for several hours. I don't know where they went. She had an odd look on her face when she returned, though."

"Did something happen while she was with him?"

"She asked me to prepare a bath, an odd request, for she'd bathed that morning. But the roads were dusty, and she wanted to wash it off. Afterwards, she sat at her dressing table, stared at the mirror, and said the oddest thing."

"What?"

"It's done."

"What was done?"

"I don't know, Miss, she didn't say."

CHAPTER 26

PROGRESS IS MADE

Early afternoon, I returned to Margaret's home to find a telegram from Hollingsworth. He'd arrived in Plymouth the day before and had booked rooms at the same hotel we'd stayed. He'd arranged to have dinner with some seafaring friends who lived in Plymouth. They knew the reverend and would provide Hollingsworth with their opinion of him. He would return to Oxford the following day.

"Goodness, he works fast."

"He would," Margaret said. "Would you like to hear my news?"

"Yes, of course."

"I contacted Mister Staunton. He's agreed to talk to me tomorrow at two. Sebastian will meet with Professor Burgess this evening at his home. Apparently, he doesn't wish personal matters to interfere with his academic life."

"In other words, he doesn't want anyone at the university to know he's talking to Sebastian."

"Seems that way. But can you really blame him? He's achieved a prestigious position at Oxford. A whiff of scandal could jeopardize his standing."

"You'd think he'd want to discover the identity of Ellen Clarkson's murderer. After all, he was good friends with her father."

"Maybe he thinks the killer has already been found."

I stared at her. "Surely, he doesn't believe Robert killed Ellen."

"He wouldn't be the only one, Kitty. Many do."

"But that's outrageous. Robert would have never done such a thing."

"People don't know him as well as you do. Keep that in mind as you move forward. You will encounter closed minds."

I sighed. "You're right. Some people will judge Robert guilty. Thank heaven Molly Devine is not one of them."

"What did she say?"

I shared what Ellen's maid had told me.

"So Professor Burgess escorted Ellen somewhere, and they were gone for several hours."

"That's what she said. When Sebastian talks to him tonight, have him find out where they went."

"Professor Burgess may very well not answer that particular question."

"I think he will. He would want to be seen as cooperating."

"He could lie."

"If he does, it could be disproven. Or at least I hope it could be. After so many years, it might be difficult to find out where they went."

"Sebastian also obtained Thomas Holland's particulars in

London. He's a barrister at Lincoln Inn's Court. I telephoned your agency and provided that information to Lady Aurelia. She will visit him. Lady Delphine arranged several meetings tomorrow with some of her father's business acquaintances to discuss the Northern Bank & Trust matter."

"Salverton is doing the same on his end." He'd informed me while I was busy hanging on for dear life. My stomach rumbled reminding me I needed to be fed. "I need food. All I've had is elderberry wine and biscuits."

"I'll have a maid bring a tray to your room. May I suggest a bath before you eat?"

"I am rather dusty, aren't I?"

"Among other things."

I caught my reflection in the hall mirror. Good heavens, my hair looked like a bird's nest.

"Didn't you wear a hat?"

"I lost it. Don't ever get into a motorcar with Salverton if you value your life."

I left her laughing while I proceeded up the stairs.

After I bathed and changed my clothes, a luncheon tray was brought to me. As before, it was elegantly presented with yet another rose in a silver bud vase. As I was finishing the meal, a knock sounded on my door. "Come in."

"Another telegram." Margaret handed me the envelope which I quickly opened.

"It's from Sir Frederick Stone." I read it out loud.

"Thomas Holland is a fine barrister.
He has no connection to this murder.
Stop enquiring into his life."

"How on earth did he even find out?" I asked, tossing the message on the table.

"Someone from your agency must have called Mister

Holland to get an appointment with him. The legal fraternity is a small, tight-knit community. He must have known Sir Frederick was Robert's barrister. More than likely, he telephoned Sir Frederick to ask why he was being approached."

As it turned out, Margaret was right.

Lady Aurelia telephoned later that afternoon. She'd managed to talk to Thomas Holland. "He had only a few minutes to spare since he was due in court. He swears he knows nothing at all about the murder. He explained Ellen was the infatuation of a young man. When she promised herself to Robert Crawford, he didn't pursue her any further. He's now married with two young children. I verified the latter after I met with him."

"His current happy-family-man status doesn't preclude him from having murdered Ellen Clarkson when he was a younger lad."

"The thing of it is, though, he was quite ill at the end of Michaelmas term. So much so, he was admitted to Horton Hospital. If that can be verified at your end, it would appear he can be stricken off the list of suspects."

"I'll do that. Thank you, Lady Aurelia. How are matters at the agency?"

"Rather slow. I'm knitting booties for the Foundling Home."

I had to laugh.

"I've been thinking of turning in my resignation."

"Why?"

"I hate to take a salary under false pretenses."

"Nonsense. Things will turn around. You'll see. Or do you have another reason for wishing to resign?"

"Oh, no. Everyone's been lovely, and the work has indeed been interesting. I just hate not being useful."

"But you are. I'm sure those babies will appreciate your efforts."

"Thank you for saying that."

"Is Lady Emma there?"

"She's gone to meet Mary Perlmutter."

"Can you have her telephone me when she returns?"

"I believe she'll be returning to Worthington Manor. Lord Marlowe has invited her to the theatre and a late supper. Should I leave word for her to call you from there?"

"No." Lady Emma was entitled to a personal life. She couldn't be expected to put it on hold because mine was in shambles. "Have her telephone me tomorrow when she arrives at the agency."

"Very well."

I hung up, ecstatic and deflated at the same time. We were moving forward. We just had to gather all the pieces.

CHAPTER 27

SECOND MEETING OF THE OXFORD INVESTIGATIVE COMMITTEE

The next day Margaret was off to visit Mister Staunton while I headed to the hospital to verify Thomas Holland had been treated there in 1913. I expected it to be true as it was something that could be proved. Hospitals tended to keep immaculate records. Still, it needed to be done.

I hadn't connected with Sebastian to ask him about Professor Burgess. He'd returned home after I'd gone to bed and left early this morning to attend another meeting with his colleagues. They were forming a consortium to encourage organic farming across the United Kingdom. If anybody could do it they would, as they had the support of Oxford University behind their endeavor.

Lady Delphine had sent a note. Her meetings were proceeding accordingly. Salverton said the same, although he'd phrased it another way. And Hollingsworth was on his way back from Plymouth.

Unfortunately, I'd missed Lady Emma's call. She'd telephoned while I was away. When I called her back, she wasn't there. She'd gone out to follow a lead.

That night I dined alone, as Margaret and Sebastian had been invited to a musical evening at one of their friend's homes. Margaret was no aficionado of Mozart, or any other composer for that matter. I imagined she was doing a bit of fundraising for her women's health clinic. She'd asked me if I wished to come along, but I'd developed a headache. A real one this time. So I retired to my room and hoped the next day would bring progress to our cause.

The next day, just as the second meeting of the Oxford Investigative Committee was about to start, a commotion from the front of the house alerted us to some visitors.

"Are you expecting someone?" I asked Margaret.

"Not I."

"Me neither," Sebastian said.

We didn't have long to wait as Maxwell soon appeared at the library. "Begging your pardon, Your Graces. Lady Emma, Lord Marlowe, and Mister Worthington have just arrived."

Skirting him, Lady Emma fairly flew forward to embrace me. "You don't mind our coming, do you?"

"Mind? Heavens, no. I spent the better part of yesterday trying to find you."

"Good. I brought Marlowe along."

"The more the merrier," I said with a smile.

"Kitty." Ned hugged me. "How are you?"

I couldn't lie, not to him.

"Worried. I can see." He squeezed my hand. "Hopefully, our news will ease some of it."

I certainly hoped that would be the case.

The library wasn't as large as the one at Worthington Manor. With the addition of three guests, it became rather crowded. But nobody seemed to mind. Once introductions were made, Lord Marlowe and Lady Emma sat next to each other in one of the blue settees while Margaret and Sebastian did the same in a burgundy one. Lord Salverton and Lady Delphine settled into a brown leather sofa, and Hollingsworth and Ned took possession of two matching brown leather chairs.

I'd planned the meeting in a particular order, but with the addition of the London contingent, that would not work. I provided a quick summary of what everyone had been investigating so everyone would know who would report on what. And then I decided to start with the one who'd traveled the farthest. "Hollingsworth, could you report on what you found?"

"You asked me to report on Reverend Clarkson and discover whether he was an honest man. After dinner with my friends, I'm happy to report he is. It's my belief, we can take him at his word."

"So Ellen really did tell him she'd been seduced and was returning to Oxford to confront the fiend."

"Yes," Hollingsworth responded.

"But what if she wasn't in fact seduced?" Lady Emma asked. "What if she made it up?"

"Thank you for bringing that up. I'd like to defer the discussion of that topic until after everyone has reported their findings. Otherwise, we'll never get through it all."

"Very well," Lady Emma replied.

"What about the maid who accompanied Ellen Clarkson to Oxford?" I asked.

Lady Emma retrieved the journal in which she kept her case notes. "After you asked me to investigate, I sent notes around to every domestic agency in London. I promised a small reward to the one that provided me with the particu lars of Miss Perlmutter's address. Within two days, I had the answer. I sent a note round to Miss Perlmutter. She responded she would be willing to sit down with me. Though not at her employer's. We made an appointment at a nearby tea shoppe."

"The Tea and Tattle?" I asked.

"Indeed. She was familiar with it. I promised to reimburse her for her time."

"Of course."

"She'd been asked by Reverend Clarkson to accompany his cousin, Ellen Clarkson, to Oxford. She, herself, was on her way to Birmingham to visit her family over the holiday. As Reverend Clarkson didn't wish his cousin to travel third class, he upgraded Miss Perlmutter's ticket to first class all the way to Birmingham. She was very appreciative for the trains were crowded due to the holiday."

"A nice gesture on his part," I said.

"The trip from Plymouth to London, as you know, is a five-hour ride. Miss Clarkson spent the time writing in her diary. Although she did converse with Miss Perlmutter over their luncheon, she did not reveal much."

"That's disappointing." I'd hoped she had.

"She was not likely to share confidences with a perfect stranger."

"True."

"But here's the interesting thing. After they boarded the Oxford-bound train in London, the maid asked whether anyone would be meeting her charge at the station. As she had a few minutes before her Birmingham-bound train came through, she could assist her with hailing a taxicab. Miss Clarkson said there was no need. A friend was meeting her."

"What friend?"

"Miss Clarkson did not say. But Mary wanted to ensure

her safety. So, she followed Miss Clarkson to the waiting room where a woman with hair as red as flame greeted her."

"Letitia Fairbright. It had to be her. She didn't mention this when I spoke to her."

"She wasn't happy, the woman who met Ellen. An argument broke out between them. Miss Perlmutter was so concerned, she would have followed them. But just then her train was announced. She had no recourse but to board it. She'd wondered what the disagreement had been about. Once she returned to Plymouth, she didn't hear anything had happened to Ellen. If something had, her cousin would have known. So, she didn't think any more about it until the discovery of Miss Clarkson's remains appeared in the papers. She started to write a letter to Reverend Clarkson telling him what she'd seen, but then news came about Robert's arrest. So, in the end she never sent it."

"Well, she certainly needs to tell the police now," Margaret said.

"Absolutely. I'll inform Robert's barrister, as well." I jotted and double underlined that reminder in my notebook.

"Yes, indeed," Margaret said. "Any reasonable doubt he can interject into the case against Robert can only help his defense."

"There could be a perfectly reasonable explanation as to that argument," Ned suggested.

"Well, whatever it is, Kitty will need to find out," Margaret said. "Miss Fairbright may not have lied to her, but she sinned by omission."

"Oh, I will. Tomorrow, if I can arrange it. Anything else, Lady Emma?"

"No. That's all."

"Thank you. Excellent reporting as always."

Lady Emma's cheeks turned rosy from my praise.

I turned to my brother. "Ned, tell us what you found."

Before taking the floor, he retrieved a document from the briefcase he'd brought with him. Trading places with him, I occupied his chair as there was nowhere else to sit.

"Kitty asked me to look into the matter of the Northern Bank & Trust's 'lost' funds," he said. "The basic facts are these. Fifteen years ago, 25,000 pounds disappeared from a fund that was investing in natural resources. As you can imagine, this caused quite a stir among those who'd invested in the fund. The bank found itself besieged by investors demanding answers. Ten days later, the money was found. A simple bookkeeping error, or so the bank said."

"Is that what really happened?"

"No." Ned shook his head. "The money was stolen. The British government traced the funds to Central America where it disappeared into the pockets of a politician. He needed it to finance a coup d'état. The money was never returned."

I didn't wonder how he'd gained insight into such information. During the Great War, Ned had worked for the War Department. Given the fact the money had ended up in the pockets of a Central American dictator, British national interests had been involved. More than likely, he would have known about it. And even if he hadn't, a simple request to someone in a position of power would have magically opened doors for him.

"But how did it reappear?"

"Mister Staunton, a member of the bank's board of trustees, did not wish the institution to fail. He replaced the funds with the money his wife had inherited from her father. Some of it anyway. As he'd invested her inheritance wisely, the fortune had grown to quite a considerable amount. So, the 25,000 pounds, although substantial, hardly made a dent in his wife's worth."

"That was very generous of him," I said.

"Yes, it was. He saved the bank from bankruptcy and preserved the assets of many investors. But during my investigation, I discovered something else." He took a moment to sip some water.

Hardly a breath was drawn while we waited for him to continue.

"Through the years, several large amounts were withdrawn from Mister Staunton's accounts, too large to be deemed living expenses. Curious, I investigated them." He glanced up from his notes. "The money had been transferred into his brother-in-law's account."

I gasped. "Professor Clarkson?"

"Exactly so."

"Why?"

"The answer to that question took some unraveling. So, I beg your indulgence if I seem a bit long-winded."

I doubted anyone would mind.

He glanced down at his notes once more. "The first withdrawal took place a few months after Ellen's mother passed away. She'd inherited 50,000 pounds from her father, same as her sister. Professor Clarkson depleted that amount within the nine years of their marriage."

"Good heavens," Lady Emma exclaimed. "How does one spend that much money in so short a period of time?"

"That's what piqued my curiosity," Ned said. "It took a bit of digging, but I finally found the answer." He paused for dramatic effect.

"Don't keep us in suspense, Ned," I urged.

Flashing a triumphant smile, he rocked back on his heels. "Professor Clarkson gambled."

"No," I said.

"Yes," Ned responded. "While his wife was alive, he had plenty of funds. But once that money was gone . . ."

"He borrowed from Mister Staunton," Sebastian said.

"That's what I determined. The withdrawal dates from Mister Staunton's accounts coincided with Professor Clarkson's deposits into his. This went on for years. To the tune of 30,000 pounds, all told."

Gasps circled the room.

"And then the withdrawals stopped."

"When?" Margaret asked.

"Right around the time of the theft from the Northern Bank & Trust's fund."

"Mister Staunton couldn't afford to keep handing over money to his brother-in-law when he had to replace that amount."

"That's my guess. But here's the curious thing, large deposits into Professor Clarkson's account continued."

"He took the money from his daughter's dowry," Margaret said. "The cad. How could he do that to his own daughter?"

"He needed to feed his addiction" Lady Delphine said. "It's sad, but true. Men have ruined themselves, destroyed their families, betting what they don't have on the next turn of a card."

"Not someone you know, I hope," Salverton said softly.

Lady Delphine's breath hitched. "He was a dear friend of Father's. Rather than face ruination, he ended it all."

"I'm sorry," Salverton's kind gaze spoke volumes.

Into the silence that followed, Lady Emma thankfully spoke up, "Could we adjourn for a few minutes? I need to, er, freshen up."

"Yes, of course." After Lady Delphine's emotional confession, we all needed a moment.

CHAPTER 28

SECOND MEETING OF THE OXFORD INVESTIGATIVE COMMITTEE (PART DEUX)

During the brief respite, overnight arrangements were made. Ned and Lady Emma would spend the night with us. Salverton offered his humble abode to Marlowe, a fifteen-room palatial estate from what I'd heard. Being no fool, he accepted the invitation. As it was already after four, the meeting was bound to last until early evening, so I suggested to Margaret that she should count on having all committee members for dinner.

"Already arranged, dear sister."

"How? You haven't left the room."

"Maxwell. When he showed in our London guests, he raised his brow, and I nodded. I'd already planned for six, so three more won't be a hardship."

"You should hire Maxwell for Wynchcombe Castle. He's a wonder."

"No need. We already retained a wonderful one, one Mother found, of course. Besides, we'll need Maxwell to remain here as our butler."

I scrunched my brow. "But you'll be returning to London in a couple of months."

"We plan to do so, but we'll be keeping this residence as well. Its owner was more than happy to sell once he heard Sebastian's very generous offer."

"What prompted that decision?" I was curious, to say the least.

"Since I'll be overseeing the progress of the women's health clinic and Sebastian will be participating in the organic farming consortium, we'll need a place to call home while at Oxford. If those were not enough reasons, I've been asked to chair an effort to encourage female enrollment at the university."

"Congratulations! That's quite an honor. When will that endeavor begin?"

"I'll start my recruiting efforts in the spring. London should prove fertile ground, don't you think?"

"Absolutely. There certainly will be enough ladies there for the season."

"I don't intend to limit myself to those who are well-heeled, Kitty. Oxford needs students who represent a cross section of society. We'll be establishing a scholarship fund for those who can't afford the fees."

"That's wonderful, Margaret. I'd love to help."

"Oh, don't worry." She squeezed my shoulder. "You will."

I had to laugh. "Did you ever think your life would be this full?"

"No. Truth be told, I saw myself as an academic."

"And then you fell in love."

"Yes, that tossed those plans out the window."

Sebastian sidled up to her and wrapped an arm about her waist. "You're talking about me."

They were so attuned to each other, they sensed each other's thoughts.

"I was telling Kitty about our Oxford plans."

"What do you think?" he asked me.

"I think they're perfectly splendid."

"Ahem," Lord Marlowe hinted. "Shall we resume?"

"Yes, of course." Leave it to Marlowe to issue a strong hint. But he was right. Everyone was back in their seats. Refreshments had been replenished. It was time to get going once more. "Ned, please continue."

"As we know from Reverend Clarkson's account, Ellen demanded the money from her father so she could make plans for her wedding. He must have told her there was little left."

"Five thousand pounds, according to Reverend Clarkson," Hollingsworth said.

"More than likely, they argued about it, precipitating her father's heart attack."

"Miss Devine, her maid, told me Ellen's tears were often driven by rage," I said. "That's why she was so angry. She hated her father for stealing her dowry. But she loved him as well. No wonder she fled to Plymouth. She could find some peace there." I allowed time to let that sink in. "Do you have anything else to add, Ned?"

"There was one thing that piqued my curiosity."

"And what was that?"

"No one seemed to have known about Professor Clarkson's gambling. Not even his daughter. By the huge sums he lost, you would have thought word would have gotten out."

"Well, Mister Staunton certainly knew," I said.

"But he wouldn't have wished it known that his brother-in-law was an inveterate gambler," Lady Emma said. "So, he would have kept mum about it."

"Professor Clarkson withdrew large amounts from his account almost as soon as Mister Staunton deposited them. Who benefited from those withdrawals? One person? More than one?"

"He could have bet on horses," Salverton said. "That can be a rather expensive habit."

"Maybe some, but not all. Many sums were withdrawn during months when no horse races were held. I think he lost his money at cards. Remember the Duke of Wynchcombe? Not Sebastian. His grandfather. He played for huge sums and usually won. Plenty of gentlemen owed him money."

"Are you saying Professor Clarkson played cards with the former duke?" I asked.

"No. Professor Clarkson would have never been invited to participate in those games. Sebastian's grandfather ran in quite exalted circles, and he was based in London. Professor Clarkson's station in life would not have measured up, and he resided in Oxford."

"Then who?"

"Someone within Oxford academia who's an expert at cards. Someone like Sebastian's grandfather but situated here in town and clever enough to play those kinds of games. Whoever it was, he was acquainted with Professor Clarkson. At some point, he determined the man's weakness and preyed upon it. It may have started with a simple game, no monies exchanged hands. And if they did, the amounts would have been rather small. As time passed, the stakes increased, until Professor Clarkson found himself losing much more than he won."

"It fits," I said. "We'll need to discover who it was. Mister Staunton might know. We'll need to talk to him once more."

"I'll be happy to discuss the subject with him," Margaret offered.

"No, he won't open up to a woman, not about Professor Clarkson's gambling. Ned, I hate to ask, but do you think you could? You're the one most familiar with the subject."

"Be glad to."

"Thank you. I hope Father doesn't mind you taking time away from your other responsibilities."

"On the contrary, Kitty. He wants this murder solved. So does Mother for that matter. They're both seriously worried about Robert."

As we all were, most especially me. "I think we'll also need someone local to lend his heft. Lord Salverton, could you accompany Ned? You know Oxford better than he does."

"Happy to do so," Lord Salverton answered.

"I graduated from Oxford, Kitty," Ned objected. "I'm quite familiar with the town."

My, he was prickly today. "Yes, you did, and got a first in Economics. But you've spent the last decade in London. Lord Salverton, on the other hand, not only studied at Oxford but is quite well-known around town. Mister Staunton will find it difficult to say no to him, especially after you confront him with all your facts."

"Very well," Ned said. Polite words, but I could tell he was irked.

"Thank you, Ned. I don't know what I'd do without you."

A raised brow said he'd cottoned on to my attempt to pacify him. But he said nothing more.

"All right. I believe that's all from London. Should we move on to Oxford?"

"Is there anything to drink other than coffee and tea?" Marlowe asked.

"Yes," Sebastian stood. "My apologies. I should have offered something sooner."

"Can't it wait?" I asked. "We're in the middle of a meeting."

"We won't get through it unless I have a small libation," Marlowe responded.

In other words, he would cause a scene.

"Fine. We'll take a small interlude so the gentlemen—"

Emma cleared her throat.

I glared at her. "Not you, too."

"It's been a long day, Kitty."

I glanced at my watch. "We'll reconvene in fifteen minutes." Having said that, I walked out and headed toward my room. The beginning of a headache was making itself felt. I returned at the appointed time to find everyone easily conversing. I rapped the ruler I'd fetched from my room against a table to gain their attention. "If everyone could return to their seats, we will resume."

"Let's have Lord Salverton and Lady Delphine share what they discovered. They talked to investors of the Northern Bank & Trust."

"Ladies, first," Lord Salverton said.

"Thank you." She sent him an incandescent smile, which he reciprocated. "I talked to three of father's friends, all of whom had accounts at that bank. After the debacle of the missing funds, they closed them. As Mister Worthington said, they were suspicious about the miraculous discovery of the money. They weren't comfortable leaving their funds there."

"Same here," Salverton said.

"Were they ever provided with a more in-depth explanation?"

"No," Lady Delphine said. "They only received a letter saying it was a bookkeeping error, and they had full access to their funds once more."

"Least said, soonest mended, Kitty," Ned said. "The bank

wouldn't have wanted to expand on the matter. The more you say, the easier it is to disprove."

"Very well. Margaret, you talked to Mister Staunton. What did he share with you?"

"At first, he was very reticent to talk about Ellen. But when I revealed everything we'd learned, he opened up. You were right, Ned. Ellen asked her father about her dowry. He apparently hemmed and hawed for a few weeks. That July was the final straw. Apparently, she'd bought clothes on credit, and he refused to pay the bill. When she pressed him on it, he told her the dowry was gone. She did not take the news well, and an argument broke out. It became particularly heated, and then he clutched his chest and keeled over."

"That must have been rather horrible."

"From all accounts, it was. To hear Mister Staunton say it, she had a mental breakdown. Her brother, although only fourteen years of age at the time, had the presence of mind to call him, Professor Burgess, and the doctor. The latter determined Professor Clarkson had died from a heart attack. They hushed up the details of the argument as they did not want a scandal to spread."

"And so poor Ellen grieved over a father who'd betrayed her trust while simultaneously hating what he'd done. Did she ever find out about her father's gambling?"

"I didn't ask Mister Staunton about it as I didn't know," Margaret said. "But he didn't mention it."

"Of course, he didn't. He wants no stigma attached to Professor Clarkson's memory if for no other reason than his nephew. Oliver Clarkson wouldn't deserve the shame that would have been visited on him."

"I asked him whether Ellen had received visitors. She had. Letitia Fairbright, Mrs. Swanson, Professor Burgess, and, of course, Robert, among others."

I glanced down at my notes. "How did he feel about the revelations at the inquest?"

"About Ellen's loss of virtue, you mean?" Margaret asked.

"Yes."

"He swears he knew nothing about it and insists it didn't happen under his roof."

"Can we talk about that topic now?" Lady Emma asked.

"Yes. It's time. Why do you think she was never seduced?"

"She left town to get away from her seducer. That's what she said."

"Yes."

"But then she returned a month later to confront him. Why?"

"Maybe she needed the time and space to screw her courage to the sticking place, as Shakespeare would say," Hollingsworth opined.

"I don't think that was it," Lady Emma countered. "How did she behave after her father's death?"

"She was filled with grief," I answered, "but also angry, according to her maid."

"Did her emotional state change while she was staying with her uncle?"

"Not that her maid mentioned."

"If she'd been seduced, she would have acted differently," Margaret said.

"My point exactly," Lady Emma agreed.

"Please explain, Margaret," I said.

"At the London Women's Health Clinic, I met ladies who were abused. They were fearful, nervous, avoided contact with men. Ellen seemed to have genuinely liked her Plymouth cousin."

"But she would in any instance," Lady Delphine said. "He is a man of the cloth. Someone she could trust."

"Men of the cloth have been known to seduce women,"

Margaret said. "I've heard many an account about a priest, a pastor, a minister who took advantage of the trust women placed on them. Reverend Clarkson, of course, is not like that. I don't think Ellen was seduced, but someone she knew was. That's why she was returning to Oxford. To confront the man who took advantage of an innocent woman."

I could very well guess who that woman was.

CHAPTER 29

SECOND MEETING OF THE OXFORD INVESTIGATIVE COMMITTEE (PART TROIS)

After that emotional discussion, we voted to adjourn. There was still much to discuss, but everyone was exhausted. It'd be best to defer further discussion until after supper. Since the last thing I wished to do was engage in further conversation, I retired to my room where I instructed Margaret's maid to wake me before supper. With my mind roiling, I doubted I'd be able to sleep, but to my surprise I did.

The meal was a convivial affair where everyone enjoyed themselves. The wine flowed freely, and the food was divine. But then Margaret's cook was a wonder.

It was a much more relaxed group that gathered once more in the library. Hopefully, we would finish our discussion, for I was not looking forward to starting anew in the morning. As soon as everyone had settled into their seats, I called the meeting to order.

“Let’s see, Margaret had the floor. Anything else you wished to discuss?”

“No. That was all.”

“Let’s move on to Sebastian, and his discussion with Professor Burgess.”

“At his request, we met at his home—a mansion in Headington Hill with a gated entrance into a private lane. I must say I was surprised by the opulence of the place.”

“Why so?” I asked.

“Oxford wardens, as well as masters, usually live in quarters within their colleges. It’s one of the benefits of such positions. Professor Burgess, however, resides in a large house which contains six bedchambers, according to him. The furnishings, on the ground floor at least, are of the Georgian period, and the front and back gardens are meticulously landscaped.”

“Ummm,” I said. “It will be interesting to discover how Professor Burgess came by that property. Ned?”

“I’ll look into his finances.”

“Thank you.” He could always be counted upon. Turning back to Sebastian, I asked, “So what did Professor Burgess say?”

“Nothing you wouldn’t expect. Professor Clarkson was his best friend. He grieved over his death. He was called to the house after Professor Clarkson suffered his fatal heart attack. He took on the care of Oliver, as both he and Mister Staunton thought it best, given how upset Ellen was. I asked him when he saw her last. He said it was when he visited her aunt and uncle’s house. He didn’t see or hear from her ever again.”

“Do you believe him?”

“I think he’s hiding something. There’s the subterfuge behind Professor Clarkson’s death we’ve just learned about.

But it's more than that. I can feel it in my gut." He patted his belly.

"Well, we'll just have to figure out what that is." I had a pretty good idea what he was hiding. But until it was confirmed, I did not wish to speak of it. "Anything else?"

"No. Sorry I could not be of much help."

"Oh, you have been."

"What about your discussions, Kitty?" Margaret prompted.

"I talked to Molly Devine, Ellen's maid. Lord Salverton was kind enough to escort me to her home." I fake shuddered.

Lord Hollingsworth chuckled. "You survived the trip."

"I lost my hat."

"My apologies. I'll reimburse its cost."

"No need," I answered with a smile. "I have plenty more."

"So what did Miss Devine say?" Lady Emma asked.

I shared what Ellen's maid had revealed.

"Clearly, we need to find Ellen's diaries," Margaret said.

"Underneath her mother's roses, whatever that means. I'll telephone Oliver Clarkson and beg his indulgence once more. Hopefully, he'll agree to let me search the house. I believe those diaries are the key to solving this murder."

"Don't tell him that's what you're doing," Hollingsworth warned. "He may not approve."

"Oh, I won't."

"What about Miss Fairbright?" Lady Emma asked.

I related what she'd said.

"She didn't mention that she'd met Ellen at the train station?" Margaret asked.

"No. I'll be asking her about that and other things as well."

"So Professor Burgess sponsored her matriculation into Oxford?" Lady Emma asked.

"Yes. She owes a fair amount to him."

"What if he did something to her?" Lady Delphine asked.

I didn't want to speculate about Miss Fairbright. "I think it best if we table that discussion. To start with, we don't know much more than what she told me, and second, it could harm her reputation."

Lady Delphine pinked up. "Sorry. I didn't mean . . ."

Salverton, who was closest to her, squeezed her clenched hands. "No harm done."

"Indeed. We'll find out the truth soon enough." At least, I hoped we would.

Thankfully, Margaret stepped into the awkward breach. "That is why it's so important to offer scholarships to women who don't have the financial means to attend Oxford."

"Count me in on the scholarship project. I'd like to contribute," Salverton said.

"Me too," echoed Hollingsworth.

"Thank you, both," Margaret responded.

"I'll talk to Father," Lady Delphine said. "I'm sure he'd like to donate, as well."

"That would be wonderful," Margaret said.

Lady Emma cleared her throat as she stared at Marlowe who'd been half listening, half nodding off. When that had no effect, she elbowed him hard in the ribs.

"What?" he said coming fully awake.

"We're contributing to Margaret's scholarship fund."

"Are we?" he blinked as he gazed around the room.

"Yes." She stared fixedly at him.

"Count me in," he said.

Her glare turned into a loving gaze. "Thank you, Lord Marlowe."

He brought her hand to his lips and kissed it. "My pleasure."

Lovebirds! "Now that that's settled, I'd like us to split into two groups. Ned, Lady Emma, Lords Marlowe and Salverton in one. Lord Hollingsworth, Lady Delphine, Margaret, and Sebastian in the other. I want you to make suggestions as to how we will proceed. Specifically, issues we need to investigate. People we need to talk to. We'll reconvene in half an hour."

"I'll ring for coffee," Margaret said, coming to her feet.

"Please do." We'd need it to stay awake for another hour at least.

One group remained in the library, the other withdrew to the drawing room. By the time we reconvened, they'd developed a solid plan.

Ned would investigate Professor Burgess's finances. Since that would need a trip to London, Salverton would talk to Mister Staunton about Professor Clarkson's gambling. Margaret and I would search Oliver Clarkson's home. If we found the diaries, all the ladies would congregate in the library to read them.

Which left Hollingsworth, Marlowe, and Sebastian with nothing to do. The latter had plenty to keep him occupied with his organic farming group, so I did not worry about him. I dropped a hint on Hollingsworth's ear about Marlowe. The man would need to be entertained.

I would talk to Letitia Fairbright about the rendezvous at the train station. There was also a matter that I needed to confirm with Molly Devine. She had no telephone, at least not one that I saw. I would call the church vicar and ask him to relay one question. If that answer confirmed what I'd learned, I would know the truth about Ellen Clarkson's death.

Done thankfully with the discussion, I adjourned the meeting. We would reconvene in three days' time.

The next morning, I was awakened by Sarah, Margaret's maid. A telegram had arrived from Sir Frederick Stone. Robert's trial would be held in two weeks.

CHAPTER 30

A SECOND INTERVIEW WITH MISS FAIRBRIGHT

"Thank you for seeing me, Miss Fairbright. I appreciate it," I said. Once more, we'd met in her college rooms, the ones she used to tutor her students.

"You don't have to thank me, Miss Worthington. I want to discover the truth behind Ellen's murder. Almost as much as you do, I daresay."

I doubted her desire was as great as mine. But I wasn't about to argue the point. Not when I'd need her cooperation.

"I'm glad to hear you say so. During our investigation, we discovered a rather startling fact that concerns you."

"Oh?"

"On December 20, 1913, Ellen Clarkson traveled to Oxford from Plymouth. You met her at the train station." I trusted she would speak the truth, even though her identity had not been confirmed. "Is that correct?"

Her cheeks flushed. "Yes."

"Why didn't you mention it?"

"I thought it would muddle matters, turn the police in the wrong direction. I didn't kill Ellen. She was my best friend."

I looked steadily at her, imbuing my gaze with as much kindness as I could. "Yes, she was."

She released a shaky breath. "You know?"

"About Professor Burgess? I suspected. He took advantage of you, didn't he?"

She gazed down, focusing on her clenched hands. "He was, is, a certain kind of a man. He possesses the ability to determine a person's weakness and prey upon it. Mine, of course, was my desire to be educated at Oxford. I couldn't afford it, so he offered me the one thing I wished for the most, the money to attend the university. He demanded something in return."

"His pound of flesh."

She let out a bitter laugh. "How very apropos, Miss Worthington. Yes, he demanded my virginity. I could have said no, but I didn't. So, I gave him what he wanted. In return he made sure I was admitted and paid for my fees. All of them through the years I attended."

"And for three years, you were at his disposal."

"Two. The summer before my third year I thought"—she swallowed hard—"I thought I was pregnant. I told him, of course. He didn't bother me after that. He did pay my tuition, however."

A light began to glimmer. "Did you tell Ellen about the suspected pregnancy?"

She nodded. "I shouldn't have. It happened the summer her father died. But I was so upset, I had to share it with someone."

"And she was your best friend."

"Yes."

"How did she feel about it?"

"She was furious with him for taking advantage of me."

"Did she say anything?"

"She said she'd make him pay for what he'd done. I begged her not to do anything rash as I had yet to confirm whether I was with child. She complied with my wishes but only temporarily. If it turned out I was indeed expecting, she would act." She glanced down at her hands once more. "As it turned out, I was not. By the time I realized it, she'd already left for Plymouth. So, I informed her about it in a letter, impressing upon her the fact there was no need to act against Professor Burgess. She wrote back telling me she was returning to Oxford and to meet her at the station."

"What was her plan?"

"To confront him with the evidence."

"That he seduced you?" How would she have gone about such a thing?

She shook her head. "She wouldn't say what it was. All she said was that it would ruin him. He'd be finished at Oxford. She was planning to deliver the evidence to the chancellor of the university. Once she had done that, she would leave town. She said she would contact me once Professor Burgess's humiliation was complete." Her breath hitched. "She never did."

"Didn't you wonder about it?"

She jerked up her head. "Of course, I did. For months, I waited and hoped, but nothing came in the mail. Eventually, I decided she'd changed her mind and left town without confronting him but was too embarrassed to explain matters to me. That's the rationale I provided myself so I could get on with the rest of my life."

"So, Professor Burgess never approached you again?"

"Not that third year. And once I finished my studies, I did not have to please him anymore. It was degrading, but in the end, I got what I wanted. Please do not judge."

"I won't."

"Others will. As soon as the facts emerge, I'll lose my standing in the university. Everything I've gained will be lost."

"Not because of anything I say. And I can assure you all my friends and family who're helping with the investigation will keep your secret as well."

"It will get out. It's the only way to catch him. I have no doubt he killed Ellen, Miss Worthington. She confronted him and paid for it with her life." A sob escaped her. "I'm to blame for her death."

Hoping to provide some comfort, I said, "No. You're not. The person who killed her is."

She raised a tear-stricken face to me. "You're kind to say so, Miss Worthington. But I'll live with that guilt the rest of my life."

The last thing I wanted was to make her hurt anymore, but there was one more question I needed to ask. "After you met her at the train station, where did she go?"

"To her home. She needed something she'd left there. I wanted to go with her, but she refused."

"What was it?"

"She thought it best if I didn't know."

CHAPTER 31

AN EXPLORATION OF ELLEN'S HOME

Oliver Clarkson allowed me to visit his home once more. As it turned out, he couldn't be present as he had a conference to attend. He'd be gone the entire day and would return late in the evening. If I could arrive before eight, he would be glad to give me free run of the house.

To say I was delighted was an understatement. I didn't want to abuse the privilege, but I couldn't search the house by myself. So, I asked him if Margaret could join me. Going by his questioning brow, he thought it odd. But he did not deny my request. Once I mentioned my sister, the Duchess of Wynchcombe, any objections he might have had vanished into thin air.

The next morning, Margaret and I arrived bright and early at his home. After a brief discussion, he departed, leaving Margaret and me free to roam. We started in the most logical place—Ellen's bedroom. Every drawer was inspected, every nook and cranny were poked into. Under the covers, above and beneath the mattress and the bed. A chest, where she'd kept the beginnings of her trousseau. I got misty-eyed when I saw the pitiful number of items there.

"What's wrong?" Margaret asked.

"She had such high hopes for her marriage, and yet, she could only afford a few pieces of linen." I retrieved a handkerchief from the chest. "Look, she embroidered it with their initials."

"Poor thing." She said gently tracing the embroidery with her finger. "Life treated her so cruelly."

That was the moment I stopped being envious of Ellen. She might have been Robert's first love, but her life had been filled with pain and disappointment while mine had been complete with joy. Taking a deep breath, I released my resentment of the beautiful young woman whom life had treated so unkindly.

Margaret resumed our exploration, but fifteen minutes later, I called it to an end. "There's nothing here."

"I agree," Margaret said. "Let's move on to the study then."

Trying to be as neat as possible, we read every document, examined every envelope, and achieved the same level of success. In other words, we found nothing.

"I think we're going about this the wrong way," Margaret said, hands propped on her hips. "Ellen said she kept her diaries beneath her mother's roses. But there are no rosebushes. There never were."

"Which means it must be some other kind of roses. I think we need to search her mother's bedchamber."

"Her mother passed away twenty-four years ago. Would things be the same after that long a period?" She asked.

"Oliver has never changed anything in her room, indeed this whole house. I doubt he's even walked into it."

Margaret scrunched her brow. "Why?"

"Maybe he feels guilty. After all, she died giving birth to him."

"You're right. He might. Although he shouldn't. An innocent babe should never be to blame. Shall we then?"

I nodded.

Together we made our way down the corridor. Although closed doors met us every step of the way, all were easily opened. We struck gold with the third one on the right. I expected a dust-filled room, but to my surprise it was clean.

"Well, he might not have entered it, but somebody did," Margaret said.

"He mentioned a cleaning lady who does for him twice a week."

"Well, kudos to her. She's done a magnificent job." She picked up a figurine. "Not a speck of dirt on this."

Suddenly, I caught a gander of the headboard on the bed. "Margaret, look," I pointed to it.

Her brow wrinkled. "What am I supposed to be looking at?"

"The headboard. It has roses carved on it."

Her gaze widened. "And so it does."

We approached the bed from opposite sides, carefully rolled down the covers, and moved the pillows to the foot of the bed. Drawers had been built into the headboard—each about 8 inches wide and 6 inches high.

Without hesitation, I opened the one closest to me. Several notebooks were nestled there. "Eureka!" I opened one and found a childish scrawl dated January 7, 1900. Not only the start of a new year, but a new century. Ellen must have been eight at the time.

She didn't write every day. Sometimes two weeks went by without her scribbling something in it. And then she'd write furiously over a short period of time.

"We need to find the last one," Margaret said.

While most were nicely bound journals, others were rather delicate little notebooks which could easily fall apart, so we worked as carefully as we could. "We should examine the first page to check the date. Put them in order." It took but a short while to discover the most recent one, dated November 1, 1913. I started to read it.

"We don't have time for that, Kitty. What if Mister Clarkson returns?"

"He said he'd be gone the entire day."

"What if he doesn't? What if he gets suspicious and comes back early?"

"Yes, you're right. But we should read her last one and the one surrounding her father's death."

A rattle from the door reached us. In a panic, we tossed the bedspread over all the diaries just before the door creaked open.

A roly-poly of a woman, wearing a mob cap, stepped into the room carrying a mop and a bucket filled to the brim with cleaning supplies. Her gaze narrowed with suspicion when she spotted us. "What in the saints' alive are ye doing in here?"

"Mister Clarkson gave us permission," I said. "We're investigating his sister's death."

"Did he now? He said naught about it to me."

"I'm sorry he didn't inform you."

"Well, you'll need to leave. I can't have lasses mucking about when I'm trying to do my work. I take pride in it."

Margaret, of course, had an answer for that. "I can see you do, Miss—"

The cleaning lady hitched up both of her chins. "Mrs. O'Shaughnessy, if you please."

"Yes, Mrs. O'Shaughnessy. Might you be interested in a permanent position, one with free room and board? I can see your work is stellar. This room is spotless."

The cleaning lady's gaze remained narrowed with suspicion. "I might, if the coin is right."

"I can promise you it will be," Margaret assured her. "Let's go down to the study, and I'll write down my particulars. If you attend me at the address I'll give you, I can offer you a job."

Mrs. O'Shaughnessy dropped the mop and bucket, so surprised was she. "Well, will miracles never cease? I've been praying every night." She kissed the medallion that hung from her neck. "My Mickey passed on to his glory six months ago, and it's been a rather hard go, you see."

"I can imagine. Shall we?" Margaret pointed toward the door. Their voices drifted away as they strolled down the hall and down the stairs. As soon as I couldn't hear them anymore, I stripped the sheet from the bed, wrapped all the diaries in it, and tied it up with a bed sash. I gazed out the window to make sure the coast was clear. Thankfully, no one was out and about in front of the house. So I gently lowered the burden and closed the window. After making sure the room was as neat as we found it, I sauntered down the stairs where Margaret had just finished her business with the cleaning lady.

"All done?" Margaret asked.

I nodded.

"I shall see you Thursday then, Mrs. O'Shaughnessy." Margaret fetched a coin from the handbag she'd left in the hall closet and pressed it into the woman's hand. "Please hail a taxicab. I don't want you to walk."

All smiles now, the cleaning lady bobbed a curtsy. "Thank 'ee, ma'am."

"It's Your Grace, Mrs. O'Shaughnessy. My sister is the Duchess of Wynchcombe."

We left her slack-jawed and speechless as we walked out of the house.

"Are you really going to hire her?" I asked.

"Yes. Bridget, one of our maids, is returning home to marry her sweetheart. Apparently, he'd dragged his feet about marriage, so she came to Oxford to give him time to think. He did and proposed."

"Absence makes the heart grow fonder."

"Apparently. And it only took three months."

I laughed.

"So, what are we going to do with the diaries?" She asked after we'd fetched the diary bundle and climbed aboard a taxicab.

"Read them, of course. Between Ladies Emma and Delphine, you, and me, we should get through them this afternoon."

"Not the men, then."

"No. Definitely not them. Those diaries are sure to contain delicate matters."

"How will you divide them? There are a fair number of them."

"We'll have Lady Delphine read the early ones when Ellen was attending boarding school. Lady Emma can take the ones from the time she was sixteen to eighteen, and you and I can split the rest."

"Very well."

We arrived with our treasures to news of what everyone in the committee was doing. Ned had taken the early train to London to investigate Professor Burgess's finances as he couldn't very well do that from Oxford. He would return in the evening to submit his report. Salverton had arranged to meet with Mister Staunton this afternoon to discuss Professor Clarkson's gambling. Sebastian was doing research at the Bodleian library. Hollingsworth and Marlowe were visiting their old haunts hoping to pick up the latest gossip about the case. A good thing the latter was out of the house, for he could drive us all to distraction.

After Margaret and I cleaned up and donned fresh gowns, we rejoined the ladies in the library who'd put the diaries in order and numbered them. I divided them according to the plan we made while Margaret provided notebooks where we all could jot down important observations. We needed to finish our reading by late afternoon to give us time to write our individual reports. We ordered sandwiches and tea so we could eat while we read.

While Lady Delphine had the largest number of diaries—and I imagined the least interesting—she did not object to her assignment. Lady Emma busily scribbled away in the notebook Margaret had provided as she read her set. Although she made the occasional comment, she kept mum most of the time. Margaret and I, who arguably had the most interesting ones, quickly became absorbed by Ellen's narrative.

The gentlemen began drifting in, first Sebastian, then Hollingsworth and Marlowe, both of whom seemed slightly bosky, and last but not least, Salverton. We shooed them all away. Most took their dismissal with grace. You can guess who objected. It wasn't until Lady Emma shot Marlowe a 'pipe-down' glance that he finally left. The course of true love did not run smooth between those two.

As it turned out, Lady Delphine was the first one to finish, followed by Lady Emma a half hour after her. While Margaret and I finished reading, they wrote out their reports. And then we were all done. I glanced at my watch. It was 6:30 and we still had to summarize the ones we'd read. While they provided their reports, we would write ours.

Lady Delphine provided the first summary. The entries in her diaries had been rather short at the start. No wonder. They were the scribblings of a young girl with nothing much to write about. After her mother's death, Ellen had entered boarding school. That's when her entries became more interesting. She'd described her close friendship with Letitia Fairbright in much more detail than the one with Andrea Fulsome (now Mrs. Swanson). Ellen and Letitia had been the best of friends. Not so much with Andrea Fulsome, who had been rather mean. Her friendship with Miss Fairbright had helped her cope with her tragedy, and so she owed her a great deal.

Lady Emma took up the narrative once Lady Delphine was done. As we'd learned earlier, Ellen had arrived back home after boarding school to find a house in disarray. With half of the staff gone, she'd had to develop a method of applying order to chaos. To her credit, she'd largely succeeded. So much so, her father had started having gatherings, first small, and then, as she became a more proficient hostess and housekeeper, larger ones. At first, she'd taken it all in stride, but as time passed, she'd grown bitter. When she wished to attend balls and parties, her father had forbidden her. When she asked for funds to refurbish her wardrobe, her father had turned her down. All while he demanded she play hostess duties and act as his housekeeper. An unpaid servant is what she'd turned out to be.

Margaret and I provided the rest. Her drudge-filled existence took a turn for the better when she met Robert. Suddenly, her life was one filled with joy. And then everything came crashing down the summer of 1913. Much of it we already knew from our interviews, but some was surprising. The last diary entry detailed her trip back to Oxford and what she hoped to achieve. She never got to write the last chapter of her life. It would be up to me to write it for her. And that I fully intended to do.

CHAPTER 32

A MURDERER IS REVEALED

After obtaining Oliver Clarkson's permission to hold a gathering in his house with the express purpose of sharing what we'd discovered, I telephoned those closely connected with his sister and issued invitations on his behalf. On the appointed day, all interested parties were present—Professor Burgess, Mister Staunton, Reverend Clarkson, Letitia Fairbright, and, of course, Oliver Clarkson himself. I'd also asked Detective Inspector Gordon from the Oxford Constabulary and Sir Frederick Stone, Robert's barrister, to attend. I'd also invited Margaret, not only because she was my sister but because she would lend her august title if called upon. Of course, I could not leave Hollingsworth behind. He was not only a dear friend but had been a stalwart companion throughout the investigation. And, if force was needed, he was rather handy with his fists.

Once everyone had settled into their seats, I took the floor. "Thank you for coming. I appreciate your taking the time out of your precious day. You've all been very cooperative with the members of our investigative committee. We certainly appreciate your help." I paused briefly to glance at my notes. "It's been my experience that one cannot solve a murder until one understands the victim. So, the first question that needed answering was who was Ellen Clarkson?"

"My sister," Oliver Clarkson said.

"My friend," Letitia Fairbright joined in.

"My niece," Mister Staunton said followed by Reverend Clarkson, "A beautiful, kind, young woman."

"Yes, she was indeed all those things, and she was a couple more, daughter to Professor Clarkson, and fiancée to Robert Crawford."

I allowed those words to sink in.

"The thing about it is that we tend to see a person on how they relate to ourselves. Hard to see them in another role, isn't it? For example, you wouldn't have any experience on how she was affianced to Robert. He's not present, so I will speak on his behalf. I could go on and on about what he shared with me, but the end would be the same. He dearly loved her. Didn't he, Lord Hollingsworth?"

"Yes, he did."

"Lord Hollingsworth's opinion holds a great deal of weight as he was a friend of Robert's during the length of the engagement." I took a breath before I continued. "Robert was sorry the engagement ended. He would have treasured and honored Ellen through the rest of her life. It's my belief he didn't kill her."

"So, you say, Miss Hollingsworth," Inspector Gordon said. "You're prejudiced in his favor. After all, you yourself are engaged to him."

"A valid argument, sir, but as I will demonstrate, he's innocent of the charge of murder."

His upper lip curled with scorn. "How do you know this?"

"Because I know who the murderer is, and that person is right here in this room."

"No!" Letitia Fairbright rushed to her feet, as her hand went to her throat.

"Yes, indeed, Miss Fairbright." I gazed at her with as much kindness as I could. The truth would need to come out, no matter who it hurt. "If you will retake your seat, I will explain."

She collapsed into her chair.

"What about Father and his relationship with Ellen?" Oliver Clarkson asked.

"Oh, I haven't forgotten, Mister Clarkson. In a little while, I will explain."

He seemed satisfied by my answer.

"We need to know what was revealed at the inquest, so I'll recap those testimonies with a special emphasis on what the medical examiner said. Miss Clarkson was found in a makeshift grave on the grounds at Magdalen College, wrapped in a cotton shroud. He testified her skull had been bashed in. She was a lovely young woman who suffered a horrible death."

A sob escaped Miss Fairbright. "She didn't deserve such an end."

"No, she didn't. So, what happened to Ellen? How did she end up in that cold, lonely grave? For the answer to that question, we'll need to return to the summer of 1913 when a traumatic event altered the course of her life. Her father, her beloved father, died suddenly from a fatal heart attack. By all accounts, she became so prostrate with grief, she could barely function. She couldn't remain in her home alone. So, her uncle decided she should move in with him and his beloved wife, Imelda. Neither could Oliver, as he was only fourteen at the time. So, Professor Burgess offered him his home."

"It was only for a short while," Oliver explained. "I would be returning to school in two weeks."

"Yes, indeed. It was very kind of Professor Burgess to make the offer. He was not only your father's colleague, but a very good friend of his. Of course, he wanted to help his friend's son as best he could."

"I was happy to do so," Professor Burgess said.

"Indeed. And after that time, you continued to mentor Oliver, did you not? Through the years, he spent his holidays with you. You introduced him to lecturers and professors in the Astronomy Department, his field of interest, and sponsored his entrance into Oxford. By the time Oliver graduated, he was assured of a position at the university."

"I'm very grateful for his help," Oliver said.

"As you very well should be, young man," Detective Bolton exclaimed.

"But let's return to Ellen. Her grief was so profound she could not be consoled. Everyone said that, so I believe it's true. But that was not the only emotion she felt. Her maid, Molly Devine, told me Ellen's grief was often mixed with rage."

"People often are when a loved one has passed, Miss Worthington," Professor Burgess said. "I tried my best to console her, but she wouldn't accept my help."

"You visited her, didn't you, while she was residing with her uncle?"

"I did, indeed."

"Yes, that's what we learned. And then Ellen and Robert's engagement ended. A mutual decision, according to Robert."

"That hasn't been verified," Inspector Bolton said.

"I believe him." I couldn't help the curl of *my* lip.

"There is no evidence," he insisted.

"Oh, but there is," I returned.

He seemed taken aback by my statement. So was Sir Frederick Stone.

"Let us move on with the narrative. Ellen's grief was so intense, she decided to visit her aunt and cousin in Plymouth. It would provide her with space and time to come to terms with her father's death and the end of her engagement."

"That's what she said," Mister Staunton said. "I couldn't very well forbid the trip. Not in the state she was in."

"Yes, indeed, Mister Staunton. She traveled to Plymouth where she was warmly welcomed by her aunt and cousin. The following day she revealed she'd experienced a rather harrowing ordeal. She'd been seduced. Coming on the heels of her father's death, she'd become almost unhinged. Thus, she'd come to them seeking some sort of peace."

"Indeed, she did," Reverend Clarkson said.

"But then after a month, she decided to return. She told the good reverend she wanted to confront her seducer. He tried his best to talk her out of it, even asked her to marry him. But she turned him down."

"She was very kind about it."

"She was a kind person," Letitia Fairbright said, "and a true friend."

"Yes, she was that," I said. "Reverend Clarkson couldn't escort her back to Oxford. His mother had grown quite ill. But he found someone to accompany Miss Clarkson. Mary Perlmutter, a maid of a friend who was traveling to Birmingham to enjoy the Christmas holiday with her family. On December 20, 1913, he escorted Ellen Clarkson to the train station, found her compartment, and said goodbye. That was the last time anyone associated with Ellen saw her. Until a decade later when her remains were discovered in a grave on the grounds of Magdalen College."

I allowed a moment for the information to be absorbed before I continued.

"So, the question becomes what happened after she arrived at Oxford."

"That's something we'd all like to discover," Mister Staunton said.

"Well then, sir, you'd be glad to learn she was met by someone known to her."

Sir Frederick became fully alert. "Who?"

"I will reveal that in due time."

He started to object, but he must have thought better of it because he kept mum.

"This person and Ellen got into an argument right at the train station. It was witnessed by Mary Perlmutter, the maid who accompanied Ellen from Plymouth."

"Why didn't she come forward?" Sir Frederick asked.

"She did, just this week," Inspector Bolton said.

Sir Frederick whirled toward the inspector. "You have a duty to inform the accused's barrister. Why didn't you?"

"I was planning to do so when I got this summons from Miss Worthington."

I clapped my hands to draw their attention. "Gentlemen, if I could continue? I promise everything will be made right."

Sir Frederick huffed. By the look in his eye, Inspector Bolton might soon find himself demoted to Sergeant. A policeman could not withhold evidence from the legal representative of a person charged with a crime.

"This person—"

Mister Staunton came to his feet. "I demand to know who it was."

"It was me," Letitia Fairbright cried out. "I met her. She—"

"Miss Fairbright," I interrupted, "I beg you. Let me continue. There's a certain order that needs to be observed."

"Yes, of course." She sank once more into her seat.

"Miss Fairbright met Ellen at the station. Afraid Ellen would get hurt, she argued against what Ellen was about to do. But Ellen would not listen. Miss Fairbright bid her friend goodbye. She never saw her again."

Miss Fairbright sat quietly sobbing.

"Miss Worthington," Reverend Clarkson said, "please end this. We shouldn't prolong this lady's suffering."

"Only a little while longer, Reverend. So where did Ellen go after she arrived in Oxford? Why, she came to the place she knew best." I gestured to the space around me. "Home."

"Here? She came here? Why?" Mister Staunton asked.

"She needed to retrieve something her father had left for her."

"What was it?" Oliver Clarkson asked, his voice cracking with emotion.

"Her father's diary. That's what she was going to use to confront the fiend who'd driven her father to ruin. The man who got her father so deep into gambling, he lost every penny his wife had left for him, and most of the dowry Ellen's mother had placed in trust for her."

"Who was it?"

"Shall we let Professor Clarkson himself tell us?" I walked toward the bookshelves that lined the walls and reached for *The Diary of Samuel Pepys,* opened it, and found what I sought. Professor Clarkson had removed that tale and inserted his own diary. Turning back to the gathering, I read from one of the last pages, written a few days before his death.

"My darling daughter has come to me asking for her dowry so she can purchase a new wardrobe and items for her trousseau. How can I tell her I've stolen it, gambled most of it away? Many years ago, a friend took advantage of my good nature and started me on the road to perdition. Too late I came to realize he was no friend but a predator who preyed on my weakness. My shame is great. My sin is greater. Although my daughter's dowry is gone, I will one day exact a revenge. The accounting of everything he stole from me can be found within the pages of this diary. Once she marries, I will present evidence of his perfidy to the chancellor. And then, Professor Alton Burgess will be ruined, much as he has ruined me."

A red-faced Professor Burgess jumped to his feet. "It's a damn lie. Totally made up. She wrote that abomination to save her fiancé."

I allowed myself a small, satisfied smile. "It will be easy enough to validate his handwriting. There are enough of Professor Clarkson's papers on hand to compare." I'd spotted some when I searched the house.

He charged at me, but before he could get anywhere close, Hollingsworth slammed him to the ground. There Professor Burgess stayed with Hollingsworth's booted heel on his chest.

A bit dramatic, but effective.

Sir Frederick calmly asked. "What's in that diary, Miss Worthington?"

"Years of accounting entries. Professor Clarkson kept track of the monies he lost gambling to Professor Burgess. Once the handwriting is validated, the journal will be presented to the chancellor, and Professor Burgess's career at Oxford will end."

"Over a few gambling losses, ha?" Professor Burgess had been allowed to return to his seat, somewhat rumpled but still combative, with Hollingsworth towering over him.

"He was not the only one preyed upon. The diary contains evidence of others you fleeced."

"And who's going to present this information to the chancellor? You?" he sneered.

"My husband, the Duke of Wynchcombe, Sir," Margaret said. "I can assure you, his words will not be dismissed."

"Neither will mine, nor Lord Salverton's," Hollingsworth said. "You're done for, Burgess, you scurvy bilge rat." A rather unpleasant smile accompanied his words.

"Did he kill Ellen, Miss Worthington?" Letitia Fairbright asked. "Did she run into him when she came home?"

"No, he didn't." I took a deep breath. "Her brother did."

Oliver Clarkson broke down in sobs. "I'm so sorry. I didn't mean to. It just happened." He was crying so hard, I doubted I'd get much out of him. It'd be up to me to reveal what had happened that day.

"You came back to Oxford for your Christmas holiday."

"Yes." He'd been fourteen then.

"You came home to fetch something."

"One of my telescopes."

"Because you were spending the holiday at Professor Burgess's home."

He nodded and wiped his nose with his sleeve.

Taking pity on him, Reverend Clarkson handed him a handkerchief.

"You found her here."

"Y-es."

"She told you she'd received a package from your father's solicitor. In it was a letter from your father apologizing for what he'd done. He told her about the journal, where he'd hid it, told her to use it as she saw fit."

He raised a blotchy, tear-streaked face. "She was going to ruin Professor Burgess."

"And you couldn't have that. He was the key to your future. He'd already introduced you to lecturers and professors in the Astronomy Department. If he was dismissed, where would you be? You had no mother, no father."

"He had me!" Mister Staunton exclaimed. "I would have made sure he got what he needed."

"He was too young to see that." I turned back to Oliver. "You argued with Ellen, did you not?"

"Yes. She was in her room, gathering the photographs of our father, our mother, me. Oh, God!"

"What did you do, Oliver?"

"I pushed her. That's all. But her head hit the iron bedpost. I knelt next to her. Told her I was sorry. Begged her not to die. But she was gone."

Thank heaven for small favors.

"Who came up with the scheme to bury her?"

"Professor Burgess"—he hiccuped—"we wrapped Ellie in her pink bedspread. She loved it, you see. We couldn't do it right away. It was daylight. So, we waited until dark, put her in the boot of Professor Burgess's motorcar and drove to Magdalen College. It took us half the night to dig that hole."

"And then you walked away and left your sister to rot in a cold, lonely grave."

"Yes, God help me, I did. I'm so sorry. I was so young, so young."

"But you're grown now. And you would have allowed the law to hang an innocent man. I have no pity for you."

Inspector Gordon took command of the situation. "Stand up, sir."

Oliver Clarkson stumbled to his feet.

"I'm arresting you for the murder of Ellen Clarkson."

"I'm sorry. I'm so sorry." Oliver Clarkson couldn't stop blubbering.

"Lord Hollingsworth, could you bring Professor Burgess along?"

"With pleasure." Putting words to action, he yanked the professor from his chair.

"I didn't kill her. Oliver did," the professor protested as Hollingsworth dragged him by his arm.

"You helped him hide the body, did you not?" Inspector Gordon said. "That's aiding and abetting for starters. And once I read that diary, I'm sure there will be additional charges to be leveled against you." Turning to me, he held out his hand. "I'll take possession of that now, if you will, Miss Worthington?"

"Of course, Inspector." I pinned him with a hard stare as I gave it to him. "You will be releasing Robert?"

"There'll be some paperwork to get through."

Sir Frederick came to his feet. "Which I'll make sure is expedited." Approaching me, he said, "That was very cleverly done, Miss Worthington." There was a light of admiration in his eyes.

"Thank you, sir. Will Robert be released tomorrow, do you think?"

"I'll do my very best. Have you ever thought of studying jurisprudence? You'd make an excellent barrister."

"I'm quite happy in my chosen profession."

He allowed himself a small smile. "A lady detective."

"Yes."

"A very good one from what I've seen. My law offices may have need of your services now and then."

An assignment from one of the best barristers in the land would ensure the success of the Ladies of Distinction Detective Agency. "We will be glad to assist you however we can."

"I'll be in touch."

"Just—"

"Yes, I know, my dear." He patted my clenched hands. "You'll see him soon enough."

And with that I had to be satisfied.

CHAPTER 33

THE BIRDS AND THE BEES

"He's scheduled to be released tomorrow morning at ten," Hollingsworth said. He'd remained at the Oxford constabulary until the paperwork was processed, thanks in no small part to Sir Frederick who'd insisted on the prompt release. "I'll meet him at the Oxford Castle and Prison and drive him to the Prince of Wales Hotel so he can clean up."

Eager to see Robert as soon as he was free, I voiced my objection. "There's no need for him to freshen up, Hollingsworth. He can come here as soon as he's discharged."

"Kitty," Margaret said, "he'll want to bathe and don fresh clothes before he sees you." Hollingsworth had kept Robert's luggage snug and secure at Salverton's home. So, it would only be a matter of delivering it to Robert's hotel rooms.

"Yes, of course." I swallowed hard. "When can we expect you?"

"I have no idea," Hollingsworth said. "It depends on how long it takes to process him from the system."

"Surely, it can't take that long."

"Maybe. Maybe not."

I sighed. "It will be difficult to wait."

"I imagine so." Hollingsworth's gaze showed nothing but kindness.

"We'll pass the time constructively, Kitty."

"How so?"

"We can have that discussion we talked about."

"What discussion?"

"You know the one."

"Oh, yes. That one."

She curled a sisterly arm around me. "It's bound to keep your mind occupied; don't you think?"

Hollingsworth's confused gaze kept bouncing between my sister and me. But he was doomed to remain so. We would most certainly never reveal the topic.

"Thank you for bringing the news, Lord Hollingsworth," Margaret said. "We'll hold luncheon until you and Robert arrive tomorrow."

"I shall bid adieu then." One of Hollingsworth's more admirable qualities. He knew when to say goodbye.

As soon as he left, I turned to Margaret. "Can't we have that discussion now?"

"Afraid not. I must go over the supper menu with Cook. Sebastian has invited some of his former colleagues. They'll be discussing crop rotation and organic farming, among other horticultural topics."

"I think I'll have a headache this evening."

"Don't you dare! If I can put up with it, so can you."

"If I don't have a headache before, I'll surely have it after."

"It might be more interesting than you think. And Sebastian will save the most boring discussions until they retire to the library."

"Well, that's something, at least."

"Now I really must go talk to Cook. One of the gentlemen doesn't eat meat. He follows a strict vegetarian diet." She fetched a piece of paper from her pocket. "He kindly provided a list of what he enjoys."

"Heavens! Cook will not be pleased."

"On the contrary. She loves a challenge."

Supper was, if not enjoyable, interesting. Who knew a discussion about organic farming would prove to be so? The colleagues he'd invited were specifically interested in Sebastian's experiments in that regard as he'd reserved some acreage to grow those types of crops. An expensive experiment, to be sure. But he had the funds to do it. And since he would be sharing that knowledge with his fellow enthusiasts, many of whom were at the top of their profession, it was bound to attract much-needed attention to the subject.

The next morning, he left early as he was due to give a lecture on that topic at an Oxford lecture hall.

His absence gave Margaret and me the freedom to hold 'the' discussion in her private study without fear of interruption. But before we could do so, a visitor arrived.

"Miss Letitia Fairbright, Your Grace," Maxwell announced.

"Please show her in," Margaret said.

Miss Fairbright had undergone quite a transformation. Not only did she walk into the room with a lively step, but the worry lines were gone from her face. "Your Grace, Miss Worthington, I apologize for the interruption. I realize how busy you must be."

"Won't you take a seat, Miss Fairbright?" When she had done so, Margaret asked, "Shall I ring for some tea?"

"I won't be staying long. I just wanted to thank you, dear

Miss Worthington. And Your Grace, of course," she added almost as an afterthought. "You kept my secret from being revealed."

"I couldn't allow that to happen. And there really was no need to do so as Ellen's revenge involved her father's gambling."

"Even so, I can never thank you enough."

"Everything is right, then?"

"Oh, yes. Professor Burgess's arrest, it's all everyone can talk about. He's finished at the university. He will be charged?"

"Oh, yes," I said. Hollingsworth had shared with us what he'd learned at the Oxford Constabulary. "He'll be put away for a long, long time."

"I'm glad he'll never hurt another woman again." She came to her feet. "Well, I better go. I have a meeting with the warden of my college. He wants me to take on additional responsibilities."

"How wonderful for you," Margaret said. "I'm heading an endeavor to increase female enrollment at Oxford. I would love your assistance."

"I will be glad to help. Just let me know. Thank you again." And then she was gone.

"Well, that's one happy ending," I said.

"Indeed," Margaret replied. "Shall we get started?"

I folded my hands in front of me. "I'm all ears."

She described the basics, none of which was a surprise as she'd explained it all before. And then she followed it up, in excruciating detail I might add, with the importance of taking precautions to prevent an unwanted pregnancy. She not only used words but diagrams, images, charts.

"Goodness, what a lot of trouble that is."

"You'll get used to it. Once you've done it half a dozen times, it will become second nature."

"Why does it fall on the woman to take such measures? Why can't a man do the same?"

"There's nothing to say that he can't. As a matter of fact, if both methods are used, there's less chance of a pregnancy."

"Now that you've discussed that subject ad nauseam, what about the more advanced techniques of lovemaking?"

She arched a brow as she stared at me. "That's what you want to know?"

"Along with the prevention of a pregnancy. And you've covered that topic rather thoroughly. Go on," I prompted her.

"Every man is different, Kitty, just as you and I are. I imagine Robert will be quite adept at many of them. All you need do is tell him what you like and what you don't like."

That answer left me exactly nowhere. "So, is it like one from column A and another from column B? Or an amalgamation of many different things? Or does a man start at the top and work his way to the bottom?" My face heated up. "Not that bottom."

She bit back a smile. "You're making it more complicated than it is, Kitty. It's the most natural thing in the world. Remember, we wouldn't be here if Father and Mother hadn't enjoyed themselves."

"Well enough to have five children." I had to agree. "Did Mother have the discussion with you?"

She grinned. "The night before my wedding, she came to my room. Poor thing was so flustered, she hardly made any sense. I put her out of her misery by explaining that after working at the Women's Health Clinic in London I was fully familiar with the mechanics of the thing."

Now that was a surprise. "There are mechanics involved?"

"No. Well, there could be."

"What!"

"There are objects that can be employed to enhance pleasure."

"Objects? What objects?"

A clamor from the front door suddenly got my attention.

"I think they've arrived," Margaret said, looking somewhat relieved.

I rushed to my feet. But before I could run to greet Robert, Margaret stopped me. "Don't, dearest. Wait for him to come to you. Your greeting will be more private that way."

"Yes, of course."

And then, there he was at the entrance to her study. Magnificent as always, but thinner.

"You've lost weight."

"More than likely."

With a sob, I threw myself into his waiting arms.

Margaret stepped around us. "We'll hold luncheon for you. Take your time." And then she left, closing the door behind her.

"I'm sorry. I'm . . . sorry." I couldn't stop my tears from falling.

"Hush, darling. Everything's fine. I'm fine." He curled a finger under my chin and raised it. "Thanks to you."

"I was so afraid, Robert. I kept seeing you climbing the steps to the gallows. And worse."

"They don't do that anymore, you know. They have a separate chamber within the prison."

I put my fingers on his lips. "Don't. I don't want to hear anymore."

"Yes, of course. My apologies."

I couldn't stop touching his face, his arms, breathing him in. "Ummm, I missed your scent. I missed—"

He stopped my next words with his kiss. It took a few moments for the storm to die down. But when it did, he said,

"Every night I lay on my lonely cot, my every thought of you."

"As mine was of you." We kissed once more. While the earlier one had the ferocity of a wild tempest, this one possessed all the sweetness of a welcome home, as he indeed had done. For a little while, we stood taking each other in, enjoying the closeness we'd always had. But then turning away from him, I put some distance between us,. I had something to say, and I wished him to see I was serious.

"What is it, darling?" His tone had grown quite concerned.

I couldn't have that. He'd suffered enough. I swiveled back to him. Clasping my hands in front of me, I said, "I want us to marry, Robert."

His brow wrinkled in confusion. "We are already engaged, Catherine."

"I'm explaining it badly. I want us to set our wedding date. Soon."

"Oh, my dear."

I panicked from the look on his face. "You're not refusing me?"

"No. Of course not." Stepping forward, he captured my clasped hands in his own. "You've experienced some rather harrowing moments. I can't even begin to imagine what you've gone through."

"Much as you did."

"You're right. Prison was not a comfortable affair."

An understatement if ever there was one.

"But as miserable as it was, I had one bright, shining light. You. I knew you would somehow, someway discover the truth."

"I had my doubts at times."

"But you came through. You and friends and family. Hollingsworth filled me in. I have many to thank."

"Him, especially. He was tireless in his pursuit of justice."

He curled his hand over my cheek. "And you, my darling, beautiful Catherine."

"I love you, Robert. I don't know if I could exist without you, which is why I wish to marry."

"My darling. I don't want you to regret it."

"But—"

This time it was his turn to put his fingers over my lips. "Give yourself time to make that decision. You'll know when the moment is right."

I could see that he was adamant about waiting. "Very well. But I won't change my mind."

"I hope you won't. Now, shall we go have our luncheon? I must confess after weeks of prison food, I'm more than ready to enjoy a decent meal."

"Before we do, I have one question."

"Only one?" he asked with a grin.

"For now," I responded likewise.

"Ask away."

"Why did you warn me off Lord Salverton?"

"Ah, yes. Well—"

"Does he have a role in the government?"

"Ummm." He looked off into the distance.

"Never mind."

His gaze bounced back to me. "I didn't answer your question."

"You didn't have to." I didn't know what position Salverton held in the empire, but obviously it was something dangerous. Otherwise, Robert would have never mentioned him.

Threading my hand through Robert's, I led the way from the drawing room. "Now, let's go eat. You're not the only one starving."

CHAPTER 34

A TALE OF LONG AGO

The next day we traveled to London on the morning train. Within days, life returned to normal. Robert was reinstated at Scotland Yard. I resumed my duties at the Ladies of Distinction Detective Agency. When the news of Robert's innocence spread, we were once more inundated with clients.

Mother, being Mother, decided to hold a supper party to celebrate Robert's deliverance. But as it turned out, there was more than one purpose to the celebration. It seemed Lord Rutledge had something he wished to say. I didn't think much about it. As he was Robert's mentor, he probably wished to make a toast and once more assure Robert of his support.

But as it turned out, it was much more than that.

On Lord Rutledge's request, we gathered in the drawing room after supper. Thankfully, he'd recuperated from his ordeal, although he wasn't the hearty sort he'd once been.

After everyone had accommodated themselves around the room with their libation of choice, whether coffee, tea, or something stronger, he began to speak.

"You are probably wondering why I asked Edward and Mildred if I could claim your attention. The reason will become abundantly clear as you will see in due time. I beg your indulgence for the tale is long and at times convoluted."

"We're all ears, Lord Rutledge," Mother said.

"Thank you, dear lady. We'll start with my childhood."

Somebody groaned.

Lord Rutledge grinned. "Don't worry. That part won't take long. My father, the eighth marquis Rutledge, was a wonderful man and a loving father. My mother sadly passed away while I was quite young. He never remarried as he deemed his most important task was to shower me with all his attention. I attended Eton, as most young boys born of the nobility do, and later enrolled at Oxford. I excelled at both schools, of course."

A round of laughter greeted this quip.

"After my formal education ended, Father taught me about our holdings. We had substantial property in foreign parts, so I was sent abroad to manage them. India was very hot, but it truly provided me with a view of the world I would not have had otherwise. Unfortunately, after seven years I received word Father had died."

"How sad," Lady Lily murmured.

"Yes, it was. Much like me"—He patted his chest lightly—"he had a weak heart. So I put my man of business in charge of the Indian properties and returned to England to assume the title. My first order of business should have been to marry, but you see, I'd fallen in love with a beautiful lady in India. I'd proposed, but she felt England would be too cold and foreign to her. So, she chose to marry another, one of her own culture. The upshot of it was I never married. I could never love another as I'd loved her." For a moment, he seemed to lose himself in his memories while sighs from the women lent empathy to his pause.

Shaking off his melancholy, he resumed his narrative. "I had no relative to inherit the title. Our family was not a large one. So, upon my death, the marquisate would grow extant, and the property would revert to the crown. I was aware of this, but I couldn't summon the will to care."

Robert, seated next to me, searched for my hand and held it in his own. I did not wonder why. He felt Lord Rutledge's pain for he was not only his mentor but his friend.

"I'd been trained to do my best," the marquis continued. "So, I took up the reins and followed the guidelines set down by my father. Do the best you can while you can. A wonderful goal, don't you think?"

"Absolutely," Mother said.

"Time somehow flew by. Ten years, twenty years. I lived my life to the utmost, thoroughly enjoying myself. Along the way I made some wonderful friends, one of which was Edward." He nodded to Father. "Recognizing his brilliance with finances, I soon gave him the handling of mine. He also advised me to hire someone more knowledgeable about modern financial management than my former man of business. Being no fool, I did."

"Thomas Kincaid. One of my best employees," Father said.

"He proved himself so, Edward. More than you know."

"Oh?" Father remarked.

"As his first task, he performed a thorough audit of the Rutledge estate. Not satisfied with what his predecessor had done, he asked for permission to search one of the towers at Rutledge Castle. Apparently, that's where the old records were kept. Of course, I gave it to him. To my surprise, he found more than business papers. He discovered a marriage certificate. The spinster was Susan Rutland, the gentleman was my father, Robert Sinclair. Seemingly, while I was away in India, my father had married a woman from the village."

Gasps filled the room.

"You did not know?" Mother asked.

"No. And neither did anyone else, as I later discovered. For whatever reason, they traveled to a church in a remote town to conduct the ceremony." He took a deep breath, exhaled. "But that's not all Thomas found."

To say everyone was riveted to his every word was an understatement. We were all in tenterhooks waiting for what he would say next, including Robert whose grasp of my hand grew stronger.

"He found a birth certificate. A male child born of Susan Rutland and my father, Robert Sinclair. The implications were enormous. A male child born of a legal marriage could inherit the estate after I passed on to my glory. So I set about finding Susan Rutland and the child. Time passes slowly in an English village. Plenty of people remembered."

"There would be," Hollingsworth said.

"It was a scandal, I was told by the local crone. Susan Rutland had been shameless the way she'd carried on with Lord Rutledge. God had punished her for her sin for she'd died in childbirth shortly after the lord's death. The babe died with her."

"Oh, heavens!" I said. "How very sad."

Robert had turned to stone, except for his hand which was squeezing mine so hard it almost hurt.

"Yes, indeed, Kitty," Lord Rutledge continued. "After hearing such awful news, I grieved the loss of a child I never met. I would have loved him, provided for him. But that could never be." He bowed his head. "But I was not satisfied with the crone's account, so I went in search of someone who hopefully would have greater knowledge. The parish vicar. Unfortunately, he'd passed on. Determined to find anyone who'd know something, I located a servant maid who'd worked for him. And in her, I met success. She knew the entire story."

"Did she?" Lady Emma asked.

"Most assuredly, my dear. Servants know everything."

A chuckle went around the room for we all knew that to be the truth.

"The child, a boy as it happened, did not die. He'd lived." A triumphant smile rolled across his lips. "After the mother perished, the midwife had secretly brought the babe to the vicar. In a village that small, he would have been branded a bastard. So, she hoped he could find someone to raise the lad far from there. Recognizing the midwife's wisdom, the vicar declared the babe had died along with his mother, and then he put the babe in the care of a wet nurse in another village. In due course, Miss Rutland was buried in the church cemetery, with no one the wiser her babe had survived. After the funeral, he traveled to London where he made enquiries. Other men of God would know of a childless couple who yearned for a babe of their own. He soon found them, and the child was brought to them."

"Oh." I gazed at Robert who was barely breathing. Others started looking at him as well.

"I was told by the maid, the gentleman was a teacher at a private school in London. So, I hired a detective to locate the couple. It didn't take long, maybe a month or so. Mr. and Mrs. Crawford and their son, Robert."

"Dear heaven," Mother exclaimed, her hands flying to her cheeks.

"Indeed, dear lady. He was the right age, an officer with the Metropolitan Police. Eager to see this brother of mine, I rushed to London. Working my contacts at Scotland Yard, I discovered he was on patrol at St. Giles the very night I arrived. Heaven knows I should have waited. But I was impatient and went in search of him. I was set upon by thieves. Robert saved me, almost losing his own life."

"You know the rest of the story. I paid for the finest doctors and medical care. Even so, it took Robert six long months to recuperate. Once he did, I convinced him to attend Oxford by suggesting he would advance faster up the police ranks with a university degree. When he graduated, the Great War had just started, so he joined the army and went off to fight. After he was once more injured, his father and I prevailed upon him to accept a position at Scotland Yard rather than return to the front. I waited until both his parents died before telling him who he was. I then settled a sum on him, as well as deeded him the Eaton Square property."

While everyone's eyes were on Robert, he raised my hand to his lips and kissed it. "Now you know."

Unable to say a word, I could only nod.

"My brother—Robert—is now the heir to the Rutledge title as well as the entire Rutledge fortune and estate. I've asked my solicitor to organize the paperwork and present them to the courts so he can be formally acknowledged. After that day, there will be no doubt in anyone's mind."

Robert came to his feet and approached Lord Rutledge, "Sir."

"Brother. My dear, dear brother." Lord Rutledge and Robert embraced.

Mother was crying. I was crying. Indeed, all the ladies had tears in their eyes. The gentlemen's eyes were suspiciously moist as well.

In unison, the men rose to shake Lord Rutledge's hand as well as Robert's. Almost on cue, Carlton entered followed by two footmen carrying buckets of champagne and flutes.

"Did you know?" I asked Mother, once everyone had a chance to celebrate.

"No. I thought Robert was his son, his illegitimate son." Her face grew quite flushed.

"Oh, Mother." Laughter escaped me as I embraced her.

"I'm happy for Lord Rutledge," she said wiping a tear from her cheek. "It must be a weight off his shoulders to finally acknowledge Robert as his brother. How he managed to keep that a secret for so long, I'll never know."

"If I had to guess, he wanted Robert to make his own way at Scotland Yard without the weight of the title. He has done so. Now, after everything that has happened, it was time to reveal all."

"Mrs. Worthington, Catherine," Robert had suddenly materialized by our side. "Lord Rutledge—"

"Your brother," Mother said.

"Yes," he nodded. "He's tiring. I'm escorting him home."

"I'll go say goodbye then," Mother said before drifting away.

Although it was obviously necessary and the right thing to do, I was disappointed. I'd wanted a private word with him. But that would have to wait. "He needs you by his side, now more than ever."

Robert tweaked my chin, a tender gesture of his. "I'll return, Catherine, so we can say a proper goodnight."

"I'll wait up. But don't hurry on my account. Take your time."

Soon, everyone was saying goodnight. Some left for their homes. Others retired to their beds at Worthington Manor. And then it was just me and the ticktock of the clock on the mantel marking time.

CHAPTER 35

ALL'S WELL THAT ENDS WELL

I awakened to Robert touching my shoulder. It seems I'd fallen asleep on the drawing room sofa. "You're back," I said somewhat sleepily.

He quirked a smile. "Observant of you."

"How did you leave Lord Rutledge?"

He took a seat next to me. "Resting comfortably in the care of his nurse." Placing my bare legs on his lap—I'd removed my shoes and stockings before lying down—he started to rub the balls of my feet.

Every one of my senses came roaring to life. As the ability to carry on a conversation suddenly eluded me, I fought hard to marshal my thoughts. "He seems to be doing better, don't you think?"

He, on the other hand, had no such trouble speaking as he moved to the arch of my foot. "He is, I'm glad to say. His physician prescribed a new elixir which is doing wonders for him. As long as he gives up his cigars and follows a prescribed diet, he should live a few more years. At least that's what Dr. Goodman says."

"Lord Rutledge's acknowledgement of you as his brother and heir gave him ease." Before he made a total puddle of me, I tugged my legs from his hold and sat up.

Going by his knowing smile, he knew the effect he'd had on me. But then, when hadn't he? "I believe so. But he won't rest easy until I've been officially recognized by the courts. We have an appointment tomorrow with the solicitor who handled Sebastian's claim to the Wynchcombe title. Apparently, it's just a matter of presenting the right documentation —marriage and birth certificates and such."

"Speaking of which, what should I call you?"

Mischief sparked in his eyes. "My dearest love. My darling."

"That's not what I was asking."

He shrugged. "You know etiquette rules better than I do."

"Well, as the son of a marquis, you should be addressed as Lord Robert. With Sinclair as the surname. Lord Robert sounds strange to me. I'll miss Detective Inspector Crawford."

He tweaked my chin. "You can call me that anytime you wish."

"Will you remain with Scotland Yard?"

He quirked a brow. "Of course. Why would I leave?"

"How will they cope with you being a member of the nobility?"

"I'm not the first one, you know. Sir Robert Peel, after all, was the one who created the Metropolitan Police service."

"But he was the Home Secretary, not a Chief Detective Inspector. There is a difference."

He shrugged. "I expect they'll be walking on eggshells around me for a time. But once they grow accustomed to it, things should return to normal."

Somehow, I didn't think that would be the case. "When you assume the title, which I hope won't happen for a long, long while, you'll be a member of the House of Lords with the ability to influence legislation. Someone will object to your remaining employed at Scotland Yard."

"Yes, there is that," he said glancing off into the distance. "But as you say, it won't happen for a long while. There will be time enough to come to terms with it."

I let out an unladylike yawn. "My apologies." Exhaustion was making itself felt.

"You need to seek your bed. I better go."

Holding hands, we strolled toward the foyer where Carlton stood ready to lock up the house for the night.

But I didn't want to say goodnight to Robert just yet. There was one thing we needed to decide. "About what we discussed in Oxford."

"We discussed many things," he said, before kissing my hand.

"Our wedding day. I meant it, Robert. I'm ready to set the date. How about we marry in October at St. George's Hanover Square? That'll give us more than six months to plan the wedding."

He turned serious as he cradled my cheek. "Are you certain, Catherine?"

"If there's something I've learned from this last month it is to seize the day. Tomorrow is not promised to any of us. I want to be your wife, Robert, with everything that entails."

A small smile curved his lips. "Ahhh, so it's the title that finally got you to name our wedding day."

I disentangled my hand from his. "Oh, you're impossible. When have I ever yearned for a title? I'll have you know I turned down many an earl, a marquis, even a duke." I scrunched my brow. "At least I think one of them was a duke."

"And yet, you chose me."

"It's your manly charms I can't resist, Inspector Crawford." I flashed an impish smile. "Although I must say, I have seen little evidence of your physical ones. Why, I've seen more of Marlowe's bare chest than yours."

"Well, if that's a concern . . ." He raised a hand to his evening coat, unbuttoned it, did the same with his waistcoat, and then he went to work on his shirt studs. But before I could gain a peek, he stopped. "Come to think of it, I better not. I wouldn't want Carlton to succumb to manly blushes."

Carlton's shoulders were shaking with repressed mirth.

"Somehow, I think he'll survive. Go on."

"What about your mother? Surely, she wouldn't think it appropriate for your fiancé to strip in the foyer."

"She's retired for the night. And even if she hadn't, she's given birth to five children, Inspector. I'm sure she's seen Father's manly charms."

"Ahhh, but she hasn't seen mine." He started to set himself back to rights.

'You're a horrible tease, Robert."

"The better to tempt you with, my dear. After all, you need something to look forward to on our wedding night."

"That's it," I huffed. "We're going to Brighton in August. The season will be over by then. You'll wear a bathing suit, so I can finally view that manly chest of yours."

One of his expressive brows arched. "Brighton in August. Our wedding in October. Pray tell, what other plans do you have for us?"

Wrapping my arms around his waist, I whispered, "The rest of our lives."

A tender smile bloomed across his lips. "Carlton?" he said.

"Yes, milord."

"I'm going to kiss your mistress. Kindly turn around."

He barely waited for Carlton to do so before his lips met mine. And then the whole world drifted away.

* * *

DID you enjoy **Murder at Oxford**? Read on to discover Kitty Worthington's next adventure.

Murder at the Jazz Club

Kitty Worthington is thrilled to celebrate her birthday at London's swankiest club. Dinner and dancing to the city's hottest jazz band make for an unforgettable evening. And that's before a dead body drops.

London 1924. After solving a difficult murder, **Kitty Worthington** has become all the rage. Purloined Poodle? Kitty will find it. Nicked necklace? Kitty will get it back. Suspicious suitor? Kitty will make enquiries. A victim of her own success, she's eagerly looking forward to her birthday celebration at Gennaro's, London's swankiest jazz club. Dinner with friends and dancing with her intended to the music of the band and chanteuse who've taken the city by storm.

But as the singer's smoky voice commands everyone's attention, an argument erupts between the songbird's brother and a marquis. Before long, the aristocrat winds up dead, and the brother's arrested. Wrongfully, his sister claims as she begs Kitty to investigate.

The last thing Kitty needs is yet another investigation. But there's something about the arrest that doesn't sit right with her. Determined to get to the truth, Kitty and her band of sleuths start searching for answers. Soon, they discover an intrigue that implicates a high-ranking noble and a royal personage as well.

In no time at all, that scoop finds its way to the press, and threats start to mount against Kitty and her friends. Can they divine a solution before someone else ends up dead?

Murder at the Jazz Club, Book 7 in The Kitty Worthington Mysteries. A 1920s historical cozy mystery set in the London jazz scene and the highest echelon of British society is sure to please lovers of Agatha Christie and Downton Abbey. Available exclusively at Amazon.

* * *

HAVE you read the first Kitty Worthington Mystery? **Murder on the Golden Arrow**, Book 1 in the Kitty Worthington Mysteries, is available on Amazon and Kindle Unlimited

What's a bright young woman to do when her brother becomes the main suspect in a murder? Why, solve the case of course.

England. 1923. After a year away at finishing school where she learned etiquette, deportment, and the difference between a salad fork and a fish one, Kitty Worthington is eager to return home. But minutes after she and her brother Ned board the Golden Arrow, the unthinkable happens. A woman with a mysterious connection to her brother is poisoned, and the murderer can only be someone aboard the train.

When Scotland Yard hones in on Ned as the main suspect, Kitty sets out to investigate. Not an easy thing to do while juggling the demands of her debut season and a mother intent on finding a suitable, aristocratic husband for her.

With the aid of her maid, two noble beaus, and a flatulent basset hound named Sir Winston, Kitty treads a fearless path through the glamorous world of high society and London's dark underbelly to find the murderer. For if she fails, the insufferable Inspector Crawford will most surely hang a noose around her brother's neck.

Murder on the Golden Arrow, Book 1 in The Kitty Worthington Mysteries. A historical cozy mystery filled with dodgy suspects, a dastardly villain, and an intrepid heroine sure to win your heart. Available on Amazon and Kindle Unlimited

CAST OF CHARACTERS

Kitty Worthington - Our amateur sleuth

The Worthington Family

Mildred Worthington - Kitty's mother

Edward Worthington - Kitty's father

Ned Worthington - Kitty's oldest brother

Richard Worthington - Kitty's next older brother, in Egypt

The Worthington Household

Grace - Kitty's Maid

Carlton - The family butler

Neville - The family chauffeur and Betsy's beau

Sir Winston - Family's beloved basset hound

The Ladies of Distinction Detective Agency

Lady Emma Carlyle - Kitty's friend and partner in the Ladies of Distinction Detective Agency

Lady Aurelia Holmes

Betsy Robson - Receptionist and assistant at the Ladies of Distinction Detective Agency, formerly Kitty's maid

Owen Clapham - former Scotland Yard detective inspector, now employee of the agency

The Wynchcombe Family and Household

His Grace the Duke of Wynchcombe, Sebastian Dalrymple - married to Margaret, Kitty's sister

Her Grace the Duchess of Wynchcombe, Margaret Dalrymple - Kitty's older sister, now married to the Duke of Wynchcombe

Lady Lily Dalrymple - Sebastian's sister

Maxwell - Margaret's Oxford butler

Other Notable Characters

Robert Crawford, Chief Detective Inspector at Scotland Yard and Kitty's fiancé

Lord Hollingsworth - A Marquis, Explorer and Adventurer. A friend of Robert Crawford

Lady Melissande - Lord Hollingsworth's sister, now residing at Worthington Manor

Lord Marlowe - An Earl. Attracted to Lady Emma

Lord Salverton - A Marquis. Friend of Lord Hollingsworth

Oxford Characters

Detective Inspector Gordon from the Oxford Constabulary

Ellen Clarkson - the murder victim

Reverend Edwin Clarkson - Ellen's cousin

Oliver Clarkson - Ellen's brother

Professor Alton Burgess - friend of the Clarkson family, and now warden of St. Simpson College at Oxford

William Staunton - Ellen Clarkson's uncle

Mrs. Swanson - friend of Ellen Clarkson

Letitia Fairbright - friend of Ellen Clarkson

Lady Rawlston - Margaret's next-door neighbor, in search of a husband for her daughter

Lady Delphine - Lady Rawlston's daughter

Molly Devine - Ellen Clarkson's former maid

Mary Perlmutter - maid who accompanied Ellen to Oxford

Sir Frederick Stone – Robert's Barrister

ISBN-13: (Ebook) 978-1-943321-19-3

ISBN-13: (Print) 978-1-943321-21-6

Hearts Afire Publishing

First Edition: March 2023